Bickie's Thunder Egg

By
Bert Rhoads

TEACH Services, Inc.
P U B L I S H I N G
www.TEACHServices.com

Copyright © 2005 TEACH Services, Inc.
ISBN-13: 978-1-57258-375-7
Library of Congress Control Number: 2005939225

Published by

TEACH Services, Inc.

P U B L I S H I N G

www.TEACHServices.com

Contents

Mother wrapped the boys tighter in the thick quilts.

Chapter 1

Bickie's Escape From the Fire

THE MARCH WIND HOWLED through a grove of leafless maples back of the little house on an Iowa homestead. It caught at the naked rose vine on the front porch and jerked it back and forth making a thumping sound against the window.

Bickie Ross heard the moaning wind and the bump-bump of the shaken vine. He felt the icy chill of the tiny bedroom and a thick choking odor filled his nostrils. He sneezed. Then he pulled the heavy quilts over his head to shut out the cold rest-disturbing air. It was easier to breathe under the covers. He snuggled up to his younger brother, Tommie, and drifted slowly back to sleep.

Then the quilts were thrown back. The freezing air struck Bickie through his thin nightshirt. A strange brightness shown in the room and a crackling spitting noise seemed to be marching toward him from some place very near.

In the weird dancing light he made out a burly figure dressed in a thick overcoat with a fur collar. It was their neighbor, Red-Hog Smith.

He shouted at them, "Fire! Fire! The house is afire! Do you hear?"

He dragged them from their warm bed toward the window of the little room. With a blow of his mittened fist he smashed the inner panes and the outer storm-window. He pushed off the jagged splinters of broken glass around the frame.

Bickie heard Mother's voice calling his name and Tommie's. The voice came from outside and it was hardly Mother's voice, so wild and afraid.

Red-Hog snatched up all the quilts, together with the featherbed and the cornshuck tick under it. He shoved all the bedding through the smashed window. Then he grabbed Bickie and dropped him out. Tommie landed on top of Bickie an instant later.

The boys, having landed on the pile of feathers, pillows and quilts were not hurt, although the drop was twelve feet or more. Mother's arms reached for them, "Oh Bickie! Oh Tommie!" she cried and pulled them back from the house. "Pull this stuff away!" Red-Hog shouted at them, "Get it over there on the snowbank away from the wall."

Red-Hog was flinging things out the window helter-skelter. They dragged at the pile until it was several yards from the house. Then Mother made the boys stand on the still-warm covers, for the snow chilled their bare feet.

"It's all right. Don't cry!" She held them close again. "We are all safe!" Then Bickie saw that Mother had on her old coat over her nightie. Her feet were bare, too. She ran back toward the burning building.

Red-Hog Smith dropped from the broken window and ran after her. He laid a firm hand on her shoulder.

"No, no, Mrs. Ross!" He shouted in a great voice, "It's no use—pity about the house, but it's gone now. No use risking your life. Look, we saved all the bedding and quite a few other things—even the clock." He pointed to the pile of things on the snow.

When every thing was pulled back away from the house Red-Hog Smith led Mother back to the quilts where the boys huddled together under the covers.

"You wait here a minute till I look to the granary and the barn. They're far enough away. I don't think they'll catch; but I want to be sure." He turned to look at the house again.

It was all ablaze now. Fire poured from every window. While they looked the roof fell in with a heavy crash. Although Bickie felt the breath of the hot fire on his face he was cold, bitterly cold. His feet and hands were numb.

"Wait here," Red-Hog told them again. "I'll just have a look around and then I'll bring in the sled and take you all over to my place. John won't be home till tomorrow, will he?"

Then Bickie remembered that his big brother, John, was in Marshalltown, twelve miles away.

Mother stood there in the light from the burning house. It glinted on her long black hair. "No, no, John won't be home—he won't be home—what is today, anyway."

Bickie had never seen his mother so agitated.

Red-Hog unbuttoned his overcoat, reached into the pocket of his jeans and drew out a thick silver watch. He looked at it.

"Just twelve o'clock, midnight!" He shook the watch a little looking hard at it as though he couldn't believe what it said, "Seems to me like it ought to be later than that! "

He put the watch back in his pocket. "If I hadn't seen the fire coming through the roof you would all have been burned alive!"

Mother wrapped the boys tighter in the thick quilts and snuggled them close to her in the feather-bed while RedHog walked back to the barn and the granary.

"It is God's great mercy," she said, "I was sound asleep—we were all asleep. If Red-Hog hadn't been going by—if he hadn't seen the fire!...Let us thank God!"

Bickie could see the dark shape of the sled and the two white horses out in the road where Red-Hog had left them. Now he saw the big farmer open the gate. He led the horses through into the yard. He brought them right up to the spot where the boys shivered under the load of quilts.

They all got into the sled. Red-Hog slapped the lines along the horse's backs and they streaked off over the snow toward the Smith house, two miles down the road toward the open country east of State Center, Iowa.

"I was just coming home from that school meeting," Red-Hog explained as his wife hurried about getting warm soap stones and rubbing the boy's cold feet. "It was a lucky thing I saw that fire—a lucky thing!"

Mrs. Smith made a bed for Bickie and Tommie on the floor of the little parlor and the two boys settled themselves under the warm covers, but Bickie could not sleep. He kept remembering how the fire came billowing out of the house—their own house, the only house he had ever lived in. The crash of the roof into the flaming building still sounded in his ears.

"Are you asleep, Tommie," he whispered.

"No, of course not," Tommie drew himself up on his elbow, "I don't feel sleepy at all. Do you suppose we will live here at Red-Hog's house now?"

Bickie thought about this for awhile, "Maybe they will build our house again."

"Who will?"

"Oh maybe John and—and—maybe Red-Hog would help and maybe Mr. Whitney, Nels and Pete's father."

"I heard Mama say that our house cost fifteen hundred dollars to build and I guess none of us have enough money to build it again " Tommie lay down again and shuffled his pillow to make it more comfortable.

"If Father was alive..." Bickie began.

"But Father is dead. Uncle Dirk is dead," Tommie said. "That means they won't ever come back to help us, not ever any more."

The boys didn't talk any more because they knew they might cry if they did and they were both too big to cry. Bickie was nine and Tommie seven.

Bickie remembered so many things about the house. Now that it was burned it seemed more important, somehow. Uncle Dirk had built the house when he came back from California four years before the war. He had been in California almost ten years. He went out with the forty-niners. Of course Bickie couldn't remember so far back, but he knew because he had heard Mother tell about it so many times.

Bickie didn't even remember when the house was built. He had been born in the house. And now it was burned—all burned up!

The house was not big, but it was good. Bickie shut his eyes. He could see how nice the house looked with the yellow rose vine over the front porch and the two tiny windows that opened out of the garret over the porch roof. Of course no one ever went up into the garret, but the little windows looked nice from the front.

There was a cellar under the house too. It was walled with red sand-stone. All the foundations of the house were of the red sand-stone and the cellar floor had boards laid on it to make it nice.

Then while Bickie was still small the war had come. Father and Uncle Dirk both marched away with the Union soldiers. John was hardly old enough to manage the little farm, even with Mother's help. Tommie was just a tiny baby then. And now—now, Bickie ached at the thought, Hake Collins had more to say about the farm than anyone else. Bickie hadn't known exactly why, but Mother said it was because of the "mortgage." She explained what a "mortgage" was and now Bickie understood that whenever they harvested any grain or sold a hog or a calf Hake Collins would be there to take the money. He knew there was no money left for them to buy food and clothing like other people had. So Mother went out to nurse sick people and sometimes she took in washing to get money for food.

Bickie wondered what Hake Collins would say about the fire—Hake Collins with his long sharp nose, his bald head and his thin mouth that always looked like he had just been sucking on something or was about to begin.

Bickie knew from Tommie's breathing that he was asleep at last, but for him sleep would not come and finally it was morning.

Most of the boys' clothing had been saved from the fire. Red-Hog had thrown all the clothing and bedding he could find out of the window. Several old trunks of Mother's were stored in the granary. There were some extra quilts and blankets in them.

Early the following morning Red-Hog went over and picked up what clothes he could find and later they all went over in the sled to see the ruins of the house and plan what to do.

"I know what!" Mother looked like herself for the first time since the fire, "We can use the granary for a house!"

"It'll be too cold," Red-Hog objected, "You'll all freeze in that drafty place."

"John and the boys can chink up the cracks," Mother said, "After all, it's the middle of March. The snow will soon be gone. Next month spring will begin."

"Well, just as you say, Ma'am." Red-Hog pulled at his thick beard, "I guess the neighbors will help get some furniture together. You can have the cook stove out of our wash house. It's big and in pretty good shape—has a good oven, too."

They were all standing there looking over the granary and planning about it when John drove into the yard. Bickie had never seen his older brother so pale and worried. He came toward them, his lips twitching and his eyes dark and hurt.

"Mother, Mother!" he threw his arms about her, "Are you all right? How did it ever happen?"

Then Mother explained how Red-Hog had passed by and seen the fire and wakened them. "I suppose the fire may have started from the chimney. We were keeping up a fire because it was so cold."

"What are we going to do now?" John still kept his arm around Mother. "We will fix up the granary and live in that. Don't you think that is a fine idea?"

Bickie saw John's face brighten, "Of course that's a fine idea. We can fix it up so it will be comfortable. I'll bank it and chink up the walls. Bick and Tom will help and..."

They all looked up at the sound of wheels. A rig was coming down the road from the east at a good fast clip. One glance and Bickie knew it was Hake Collins. He went over and stood close to Mother. He saw John's face harden and his heavy jaw set in a determined line. John looked grown up when his face got stiff like that. Although he wasn't any taller than Mother he was sixteen, and that is a good age for a boy.

Hake tied his horse to a post in front of the gate and came hurrying toward them, his face twisted into a scowl. His close-set eyes studied the ruins of the burned house. His thin mouth quivered with excitement.

"Mrs. Ross, John," he began, and his voice was hard. "This cuts down my security to almost nothing!"

"We didn't burn it on purpose." John took one step toward Hake, "We need it worse than you do."

"Don't be sassing me, young-un!" Hake's words bubbled and sputtered as he spoke them like they were coming up out of a hot kettle. "Either you get this house put up again as good as it was before or you get fixed to pay me what you owe!"

Then Red-Hog Smith spoke up, "I wouldn't be too hard on Mrs. Ross." He said in his friendly voice, "John, here, is a hard workin feller. He'll pay you every cent of that $300, I'm sure, if you give him a little time."

"This is none of your put-in!" Hake shook his finger in Red-Hog's face and the finger trembled. Bickie watched it, fascinated. "You tend to your business and I'll tend to mine!"

Hake reached out to take hold of John's shoulder, but Red-Hog stepped between them. He towered over Hake. He thrust his big hands in his overcoat pockets and stood glaring down at the smaller man.

"Go home!" he roared. "Go home, Hake Collins. If I hear of you bothering Mrs. Ross again, I'll break every bone in your body!"

Before the week was over the Ross family were moved into the granary. The neighbors were generous with

dishes, pots and pans and a few pieces of furniture—enough to make the place comfortable. There was
even a bureau and a washstand.

John began building a lean-to along the back side of
the granary. It would make an extra bedroom for the
three boys. He also built a rude partition through the
granary dividing it into a large kitchen and a small front
bedroom for Mother. He found some old lumber in the
barn and built three bedsteads.

The old Seth Thomas clock, miraculously saved from
the fire, hung on the wall over the kitchen table and it
ticked off the hours of that spring and early summer
until June came. School was over and Bickie spent long
days playing with Tommie in the maple grove back of the
granary.

To the side and a little nearer the road the ruin of the
burned house stood, black and crumbled, while around
it the weeds grew thick and tall. The yellow rose vine in
front had been burned badly, but now it was sending up
strong new shoots. Mother had scraped the ashes away
from it and tended it carefully.

"Who knows?" she said to the boys, as she drove a
strong stake for the new vine to climb. "Some day we
might build another house right here on this foundation.
Then the rose vine will be all ready to train over the
porch again."

"I don't think there were ever any birds big enough to lay an egg like this."

Chapter 2

The Buried Stone

THE GROWING corn on the Rosses' south twenty acres was already knee-high when John walked through it. Bickie and Tommie could crawl along the green rows and be almost hidden from sight.

There was no potato patch this year. "No seed potatoes," John told the younger boys when he heard them talking about it. "Lucky to be able to get seed corn. We have to have that for the mortgage, you know."

It was the middle of July and the corn was "laid by." John began to clear away the charred planks where the old house had burned. He piled all that could be used for firewood back of the granary. He cleared the rubble and ashes from the cellar. At last there was nothing left but the sandstone walls of the cellar and the foundations.

This made a fine playhouse for the boys. The cellar door still hung from its iron hinges and Bickie spent pleasant hours playing with Tommie at "Pirate," "Goldminer" and "Treasure-dig." Sometimes the open cellar became the lair of lions and tigers and fierce wild elephants who burst forth on the countryside to do great damage on the willow hedge and the elderberry bushes, and then scampered back to their den.

It was a warm Monday morning near the end of July. The two boys played in the cellar. It was a little cooler there. They took up the charred boards from the dirt floor and slanted them against the wall to make a lion's den.

"Let's play 'Treasure-dig,' " Tommie suggested.

"Where shall we dig?" Bickie asked.

"Oh, let's dig right here," Tommie kicked at a whiter spot in the cellar floor.

Both boys dug for a few minutes. They could not dig into the spot Tommie had pointed out. It was too hard. They clawed up the dirt around it.

"Go to the barn and get the old axe handle behind the door," Bickie urged Tommie. "This must be a rock and we need something to pry it with." He looked down at the hole they had made.

Tommie ran for the axe handle and came back breathless. "Now, you pry against it with the axe handle while I I push from this side. Maybe we can get it out."

Both boys knelt beside the hole and examined the thing they were trying to dig out. It looked like a huge grey egg about fourteen inches long and certainly a couple feet around its fattest part.

"What do you think it is?" Bickie tapped it with the axe handle.

"It's a stone, that's what it is!" Tommie pried and pushed and tugged with the help of the ash axe handle.

"I know it's a stone, but did you ever see a stone like that before?"

"No, but there's lots of stones I never saw. I s'pose ther's millions of stones you never saw, too." Tommie was tired. He sat down in the midst of the dirt they had thrown out and looked at Bickie.

"It isn't a very pretty stone." Bickie kicked at the rock still partly embedded in the earth. "I can't see why it's so hard to dig up either. It looks quite smooth—all of it that we can see. You don't suppose it has roots or something?"

"No." Tommie began clawing more dirt away from the stone. "It hasn't got roots, but it's awful heavy, that's what!"

Bickie looked straight up at the sky above them. The sun shone down and the air smelled of clover and dandelions and ragweed.

"Well, I hope we can get it out," he said. "We'll scrub it off and take it into our bedroom. We can have fun with it—such a queer looking stone!"

"I wonder how it came to be buried here in the cellar floor." Tommie was using the pry again. He heaved and pressed on the grey stone. "Maybe it was there when God made the earth or maybe it got here when the flood came and drowned everything and scattered the rocks about."

"Yes, it does look like it's always been here." Bickie took up the axe handle and with his stronger arm at the lever the stone loosened a little and rolled to one side of the hole they had dug around it.

"Look! It's looser!" Bickie shouted. "Help me lift it, Tommie!"

The two boys rolled it free of the hole and sat down to examine their prize. It actually wasn't at all pretty and it didn't even look smooth any more. It was rough and grey and egg-shaped.

"If I didn't know it was a stone, I'd think it was some big bird's egg," Bickie said. "You know, Mother told us about fish and frogs that got caught in the flood. They got buried in the ground, then they finally turned to stone—plants did too. She said they were fossils."

"I don't think there were ever any birds big enough to lay an egg like this." Tommie brushed the dirt from the stone with his shirt sleeve. "I don't think it's a fossil either. It's just a heavy old stone."

After lunch the boys went to play in the maple grove and neither of them remembered the grey stone until almost sundown.

"Maybe we ought to take our stone in the house," Tommie reminded Bickie. They ran back to the open cellar and looked at it again. "It's so heavy we will have to carry it in a basket."

"Why can't we leave it here?" Tommie sighed and squatted on the floor near the stone.

"Because Hake Smith is always prowling around here looking at everything. If he saw this funny looking stone he'd take it...."

Then Mother's supper call came clear through the evening stillness. They hurried to the house, washed up at the bench by the kitchen door and sat down to the table where big bowls of cornmeal mush steamed. Mother had set two bowls at each boy's place. One was full of yellow mush and the other was full of rich cold milk. Mother always fixed it this way in hot weather. They dipped up a spoonful of mush and dunked it in the milk to cool it. In an unbelievably short time both mush and milk bowls were empty.

"Mother, we found a stone," Bickie told her.

Mother was tall and pretty with black hair and rosy cheeks. She was almost always laughing or smiling. Bickie and Tommie knew that she was the prettiest mother in that part of Iowa.

"We found a stone that looks just like a big egg," Tommie said.

"That's fine!" Mother smiled at the boys. "If it's heavy enough you had better bring it in the house and use it to prop your bedroom door. Then you won't have to use a chair to keep it open."

"Oh, it's big enough! It's heavy," Bickie told her.

"It isn't pretty though," Tommie hesitated. "Maybe you wouldn't like it in the house."

"I saw a stone over at Red-Hog Smith's house. They use it to hold one of their doors open and they whitewashed it." Mother began to clear the supper things from the table.

"Oh, that's a good idea! When John comes home tomorrow we'll ask him to whitewash our stone and then it will look nice from the bedroom. Bickie said, "It will look more like an egg then, won't it, Tommie?"

Their brother John was in Marshalltown where he had taken a piece of machinery to be repaired. Surely he would be back tomorrow. Marshalltown was only twelve miles away and it was a large town. Bickie had been there a few times and both the boys spent hours talking about the wonders of Marshalltown.

After Bickie and Tommie finished their supper they went to bring in the big stone. They carried it in the empty cob-basket and when they laid it in the door of the lean-to bedroom Mother came to look at it.

"It is a strange looking rock, isn't it?" She turned it over and brushed her hand over its coarse surface. "It surely does look like an egg. I'm sure I never saw anything like it before."

The boys hurried to fetch the cobs and wood for the stove and water for the pail that stood on the bench. Then it was dark and they sat on the floor in the middle of Mother's new braided rag-rug with the stone between them.

"When will John be home?" Bickie asked Mother.

"Not till afternoon I think." She sat by the kitchen table dose to the oil lamp and sorted garments in the mending basket on a chair in front of her.

"I wish we could go to Marshalltown," Tommie spoke to Bickie. "Do you remember that blind man who made the music?"

"Of course I remember." Bickie could never forget that. "That's a long time ago, must be a year already. Do you remember the boy who didn't have any arms and could write so well with his toes?"

The boys talked on and on of the great and wonderful things they had seen in Marshalltown. Bickie still had a piece of paper with a Bible verse written beautifully by the boy with no arms.

"If I were in Forepaugh's Store in Marshalltown I would get some cookies and candy and some jelly...."

"No, you wouldn't." Tommie looked wistfully toward Mother. "You wouldn't buy a thing. You haven't got any money."

"Some day I will be big like John. Then I'll earn money and I'll go into Forepaugh's Store and I'll buy everything I want," Bickie declared.

Forepaugh's Store was filled with wonderful things. There were coats and suits of fine material, lamps, lanterns, saddles and food. There were barrels of crackers and big round cakes of yellow cheese, cookies and candy too and bags of rice and flour. Under the counters in the grocery department there were wooden pails of jam and jelly. There was cornmeal too. There was a great deal of cornmeal and it was not expensive. Even in State Center a mile away there was plenty of cornmeal.

Often when the boys ate their cornmeal mush they talked of the brown sugar and jelly they had seen in Forepaugh's Store a year ago. Now as they thought of

John coming home tomorrow they couldn't help wondering if he might bring a pail of jelly. He sometimes did. The jelly was very cheap.

That night as Bickie lay in his bed he remembered that they hadn't told Mother where they found the queer-shaped stone, and she hadn't asked. He decided that it didn't matter. It was just an old stone that must have been there in the cellar floor a long time.

Mother couldn't be very excited about any of the things they dug up. They had been doing it all summer. Early in the spring a story had spread about the neighborhood of a man who, on digging his cellar deeper, had discovered a chest of gold. Although Mother told them the story was probably not true, the boys began a series of frantic diggings all over the yard.

Each night they reported what they had found. They dug up a couple rusty horseshoes, an old axe head and a curry comb. All of these treasures were set out in a neat row beside their bed in the lean-to room. Tomorrow, after the whitewashing, the egg-shaped stone would take its place among them—the largest and most important of their discoveries.

It is a dreaming stone. Bickie thought to himself. Dreaming things are always good to have, because they can make a boy forget ragged clothes and cornmeal mush and many other matters.

Chapter 3

Uncle Dirk's Secret

WHEN JOHN CAME HOME from Marshalltown the next afternoon, Bickie could see, before his big brother got down from the wagon, that he was unhappy and worried about something. The two younger boys ran to open the gate and then clambered up into the back of the wagon to ride the short distance into the farm yard.

They did not shout to John that he must whitewash their stone at once. There was something in John's face that held them off. They followed him into the house.

"What is it, son?" Mother asked John as she looked up from the washtub where she was rubbing clothes. "Couldn't you get it fixed?"

"I got it fixed all right," John told her. "I met Hake Collins in town."

Bickie saw a shadow brush across Mother's face, "What did he say? John, tell me."

"He says he will foreclose the first of January if we can't raise the three hundred dollars."

John's voice hung like a cloud in the big room. Bickie looked at the open window. A cold draft must be coming through it. He felt suddenly chilly.

Mother's face lost some of its usual rosy color for a minute. Then the red flushed back into her cheeks. "John," She laid her hand, wet and wrinkled from the washing, on John's shoulder, "Even Hake Collins must have a heart. He wouldn't turn a widow woman and these little children out in January—not in January! I will go and talk to him. You are not to worry."

She had John sit down and rest while she fixed him great slabs of fried cornmeal mush.

"Hey, Bick, Tom, I forgot! Run and look under the wagon seat. There's a pail of jelly!"

The two boys rushed out the door and came back in a minute lugging the heavy wooden pail of jelly between them. John opened it and spread the lovely red jelly thick on his fried mush.

"Would you boys like some, too?" Mother asked Bickie and Tommie.

Would they? The sight of that delicious jelly melting on the slabs of mush in John's plate was too much for them. They coughed and choked out the answer that they would like some very much indeed.

With Mother singing at the washtub and the house cooling in the summer evening; with John home again and the jelly, the world seemed good again; and Bickie, seeing that John was full and in a better mood, stood by his chair.

"We want you to whitewash a stone for us," he said. "Mother says we can use it to hold the bedroom door open. We want it whitewashed like Red-Hog Smith's stone."

"Where is the stone?" John pushed back his chair and looked at Mother.

"We'll go and bring it in." Bickie and Tommie hurried into their room and brought out the egg-shaped stone.

"So, that's what you want whitewashed." John looked at the stone. "I never saw a stone like that before. Where did you find it?"

"We dug it out of the ground," Tommie spoke up. "It has been there ever since the flood. Maybe it washed over here from China or the North Pole. How do we know?"

John laughed. "Get some cornhusks and lay them here by the stove," he directed them. "We won't want whitewash to drip on Mother's clean floor."

That night after the two smaller boys were in bed, Mother and John sat in the kitchen and talked for a long time. The door was open between the lean-to bedroom and the kitchen. Bickie could hear part of what they said. He knew they were trying to figure out some way to get the money for Hake Collins. He knew that when Father died last year Mother had borrowed five hundred dollars from Hake Collins. He knew that although they had given Hake all the corn money last fall and some from hogs and calves they had sold, still there were three hundred dollars owing. The time to pay it was nearly here. Bickie knew there was no money for the payment. There would not be any until the corn was husked. That might not be enough.

"If only Dirk were here!" Bickie heard Mother say. Bickie could faintly remember Mother's only brother, Uncle Dirk. It was he who had built the little farm a mile east of State Center, Iowa. He had built the house, too. Uncle Dirk never married and he lived with them excepting the years when he was prospecting for gold in California. Uncle Dirk was a jolly fellow. He had black hair like Mother and red cheeks like hers. He was always making jokes and playing with the babies, for Bickie and Tommie were scarcely more than that when he went away.

Father and Uncle Dirk went off to the war with the Union soldiers and Uncle Dirk never came back. He died "before Vicksburg," he had heard both Father and Mother say it many times, "Before Vicksburg."

It was hard to believe that Uncle Dirk would never come back. With Father it was different. He had come home sick and wounded from his service with the Union Army and he never got well. The boys saw him grow weak and pale and finally last year he died. It was easy to believe that Father would not come back.

Then Bickie brought his wandering thoughts back. He sat up in bed and disturbed Tommie, who was already asleep. He heard Mother say something that he wanted to hear. He listened with his ears. He listened with his mouth. He listened with his heart. They were talking about Uncle Dirk.

"The last thing he said to me was, 'Fietta, there's enough money in this house to take care of you till we come back.' Then he winked at me and pointed down at the floor. You know how Dirk was. He loved mysteries and jokes."

"What do you think he meant?" John asked.

"I thought he meant that there was money hidden in the house somewhere. You know we always thought he brought home more than he let on from his mining in California." She sighed. "Well, the house is burned down now. I suppose he put it in the floor somewhere. It would be just like him. No use thinking about it any more."

"Funny he wouldn't have said anything to Father about it," John's voice came clear to Bickie's ears.

"They were separated almost immediately after they joined the army and they never saw one another again," Mother sighed again.

"Did you ever look for—for whatever he might have hidden?" Bickie could hear the eagerness in John's question.

"When your father was sick, I looked a hundred times I'm sure. I went over the floor, board by board, but none of them looked like they had ever been disturbed. I looked in the walls too and in the cellar. I looked every-where." Mother's voice dropped so he could scarcely hear, "It was then I went to Hake Collins."

Bickie lay down on his pillow again. The voices in the kitchen were quiet now. Mother and John's shadow showed for an instant in the open bedroom door and then Bickie heard him getting ready for bed in the dark.

Again the memory of the burning house rushed into Bickie's mind. Again he saw the flames bursting from the windows and heard Red-Hog Smith's huge voice booming over the crackle of the fire. He shuddered in spite of himself. It all came back so real and frightening. Yes, whatever Uncle Dirk might have hidden in the house was burned.

He tried to forget the house and the war and all the ugly worries about Hake Collins and the mortgage. He tried to forget how Mother's face had looked when she talked with John this afternoon. He tried to think what he could do to earn money. Three hundred dollars was a lot to earn before January.

It was a week later when John mentioned the matter again, "I think I'll go into Marshalltown and get work on the railroad. In five months I should earn something."

"You could never earn enough," Mother answered him. "We will have to depend mostly on the corn. If it goes sixty bushel to the acre we should get over a hundred dollars from that."

"Corn may not bring ten cents a bushel this fall." John sat by the kitchen table whittling on the leg of a little bedroom stand he was making for Mother.

"I will be able to get food for the children with the washing and nursing." Mother ironed shirts on the wooden board beside the table where the lamp stood. "Perhaps we could borrow the money somewhere else?"

"No, Mother," John's voice sounded determined. "We will not borrow any more money. We will sell the farm if we have to. Meantime we will gather every cent we can to apply on the payment. Perhaps Hake will be satisfied if we can pay most of it. At least he has given us till New Year's—five months."

"But, John, no one is buying farms now. This is the worst time of the year to sell land."

"I know, I know." John laid his work on the table. "We must trust in God."

"I won't put it off another day," Mother declared. "I'll go to see Hake Collins tomorrow."

The next day Mother put on her best black dress. She kissed the two little boys good-bye and told them to play nicely until she would come back. They watched her walk down the road. They knew she went to see Hake Collins.

The whitewashed stone stood now, holding open the door to the boy's bedroom. It looked very nice sitting there and exactly like a huge white egg. The two lads looked at it. Bickie brought a pencil and wrote "E–G–G" on it in big letters.

"Let's go and dig up some more treasure," Tommie suggested.

Bickie hesitated. He felt a deep uneasiness inside him. He knew Mother had gone to see Hake Collins about the three hundred dollars. He could see Hake with his blue eyes looking like hard marbles the boys played with at school. He could see Hake's ugly sucking mouth and his hands. Hake's hands always looked like they were twisting something. Bickie could see Mother in her old black dress and with her rosy cheeks and thick curly hair and that little smile on her face. He cringed inside. If Hake talked mean to Mother! A rush of anger swept over him. He shook Tommie's hand off his sleeve.

"Let's go down the road to meet Mother," he said. "I think she will be coming back pretty soon. When we get to the rise by the fence corner we can see almost all the way to Hake's place."

The boys started off, running until they came to the spot of higher ground where the level countryside spread out before them like a flat table.

They waited for a long time. Then they saw Mother. She was walking slowly, looking down at the yellowing grass along the roadside. Now she must be hearing their voices.

When they got near enough to see her face, Bickie thought there was a tear running down her cheek, but he couldn't be sure for her voice was merry. She opened her arms to grab them as they came pelting toward her down the dusty road.

Her voice sounded cheerful. "When we get home you boys must go and gather the eggs right away. I'm going to make a cake for supper."

Bickie's mind was relieved. The cloud of trouble that had oppressed him ever since he overheard the conversation about Uncle Dirk, vanished. He and Tommie ran skipping gaily along beside Mother until they came to the little granary-house.

Mother never mentioned anything about her talk with Hake. The days went by. The weather grew cooler.

Autumn came. John worked most of the time in Marshalltown at ten dollars a month. He would have to come home soon and husk the corn.

Twice Bickie had seen Hake Collins walking along the north fence of the cornfield. Once he saw him climb the fence and go into the corn. He snapped off an ear and husked it. Then he put it in his pocket. Bickie didn't tell Mother, but in his heart anger grew.

Chapter 4

Bickie's Soldier Coat

SEPTEMBER WAS UNUSUALLY WARM that fall. In hopes of a late snow, John put off coming home. He wanted to earn another ten dollars and perhaps the cold weather would hold off long enough so the corn wouldn't suffer.

The Ross boys, Bickie and Tommie and their close friends, Nels and Pete Whitney, played on their way to school as they scurried in and out among the clumps of sunflowers along the country road.

At noon they played ball. At recesses and after school there were games and races and wrestling matches. There was a new teacher at the Ferguson School, Miss Kittie Shrike; she looked very old to Bickie. He didn't like school. He and Tommie frolicked in the late autumn sunshine and forgot that winter would come.

It was a morning in early October when the weather changed. Bickie and Tommie had finished their breakfast of cornmeal mush and milk. They stood at the window of the kitchen room in the granary looking out at the falling snow. The big flakes filled the comers of the panes and stuck to the glass. Bickie rubbed the pane with his hand to clear away the moisture on the inside. He pressed his nose against the glass. It looked cold outdoors.

"Come boys, time to go—you'll be late if you don't hurry! "

Still Bickie lingered at the window. Never in his life had he dreaded so much to go to school.

"Get your coat, Bickie." Mother's voice urged. "It's so cold today you will need it."

"But, Mother, I don't feel cold! I'll run—it's only a little way, just a mile. We'll run won't we, Tommie?" Bickie looked at his brother.

"No, No." Mother put the last jelly sandwich in the dinner bucket. "No, Bickie, you can never run fast enough to keep warm this day. You will have to wear the coat."

Then the brown eyes grew soft and gentle. "At least it will keep you warm, Bickie."

He looked at Mother's hands all red and wrinkled from washing so many clothes. He was a little ashamed that he felt so unhappy about wearing the old coat. "Mother would get new coats for you if she could." She seemed to be reading his thoughts. "We are fortunate to have good food to eat. It was providential that those trunks were stored in the granary. Otherwise you boys wouldn't have had any coats at all." She smiled at him. "We have each other. We have a warm dry place to live and we have enough food to eat. We should be very thankful."

But Bickie didn't feel thankful. He looked at Tommie's coat. Two years ago it had belonged to him. Before that John had worn it. The night of the fire Red-Hog Smith had snatched it from the wall and thrown it out the window with other things. It was ragged and thin, but not so bright and conspicuous as the old blue coat.

He brought the despised garment from the hooks along the kitchen wall where the heavy outdoor things hung.

Mother buttoned the big brass buttons all the way up. It fit tight around Bickie's neck. When Daddy was living it had fit him tight all the way down; but Bickie at nine years, could only shuffle around in it like a pole in a heavy blue tent. It was the coat of a dashing Northern soldier. Its swallowtails dragged two inches on the floor when Bickie wore it, although he stretched himself as tall as he could. It had dragged three or four more inches last spring when he wore it a couple times after the fire, but the boy found no comfort in that.

"Let me cut the tails off." Mother turned Bickie around so she could see the back of the coat.

"No, Mother, it looks worse that way. I saw one with the tails cut off." Bickie grabbed his knit mittens and shiny dinner bucket and hurried to overtake Tommie.

The boys ran. There was no time to walk. Bickie hoped they would get there just as the school bell rang so the other children wouldn't have time to make remarks about his coat before they merged into the schoolroom.

"Oh, look!" one of the boys shouted when the two Ross boys came onto the playground. "Look, here comes the soldier!"

"How are you, Soldier?" Many voices took up the taunting words. They screamed at him and laughed, strutting around in military fashion.

Bickie's heart sank. It would be just like last spring. The new teacher stood in the door. She had been teaching at Ferguson School only a month. Miss Kitty had the bell in her hand. Bickie saw her lips twitch. She wants to laugh too, he thought bitterly; anyone would want to laugh at a boy walking into school with an old blue uniform coat dragging the tails on the ground.

The line formed and the pupils marched into the entry hall. Here the boys and girls took off their wraps and

"Oh, look!" one of the boys shouted. "Look, here comes the soldier!"

hung them on hooks along the wall. Bickie was the last one in. He looked at the row of overcoats. His old blue one stuck out from the others like a red comb on a white rooster. He paused for a minute to feel of the cloth in some of the fine coats hanging there. He knew that he could never have such a coat for his own—what with the fire and Hake Collins....

Bickie walked to his desk. One of the boys jostled him and whispered in a low voice, "Soldier! soldier!"

The children were all at their desks. Morning exercises were soon over and the first grade reading class went forward to recite. Pete Whitney, Bickie's best friend, put his foot out in the aisle and nudged Bickie's foot just enough to make him look down at his old shoe. Then he looked up at Pete. Pete's red hair was tousled all over his round head. His freckles seemed to dance over his face as he grinned and made a funny face. He held a big red onion just under his desk-top. He was scratching and tickling the onion.

Bickie remembered that the teacher, Miss Kitty, hated onions. She couldn't bear the smell, she said. Sometimes the Whitney boys brought onion sandwiches in their lunches. Bickie knew that Miss Kitty would smell this red onion of Pete's and come looking for it. Pete must be thinking the same thing. He motioned for Bickie to be ready to receive the onion.

"Children!" Miss Kitty's face drew into a scowl. "I smell onion!" She sniffed the air. "Which of you has an onion?"

The children looked at one another with big questioning eyes but no one answered the question. Pete Whitney turned clear around in his seat to look back at his older brother Nels, sitting three desks behind him.

Nels stared back at Pete with a perfectly innocent expression on his flushed face.

The first grade reading class droned on. Miss Kitty fidgeted with the things on her desk. Her grey topknot wobbled a little and the flat bow of black velvet ribbon against her throat moved up and down quite fast. Bickie remembered what Nels Whitney had told them the first day of school this fall. He explained why Miss Kitty was so thin, "She never eats onions!"

Pete still turned the red onion round and round in his hands, tearing off another layer of its skin and scratching it deeply with his sharp fingernails.

"I smell onion!" Miss Kitty got to her feet and with an angry look on her long face, she darted toward Pete Whitney's desk. He slid down as far as he could, making himself as small as possible. The chubby lad fixed his big grey eyes on the teacher's face. With his right hand he let the onion down to the floor. He pushed it gently and it rolled over toward Bickie's seat. Bickie caught it firmly between his feet.

"Hold up your hands!" the teacher commanded Pete. He held them up instantly and the whiff of onion almost strangled her. She coughed and sneezed.

"Take that disgusting onion out of your pocket!" Miss Kitty raised her hand to give a sharp cuff to Pete's ear. He dodged the blow.

"I, I haven't got it!" Pete stammered in a pretended agony of fear. He glanced toward Bickie.

"Bicknall Haverhill Ross! Hold up your hands!" the teacher cried.

Bickie's hands, being pure and clean, were held up in haste and passed inspection. After searching Pete's pockets and desk the teacher went back to the first grade reading class.

Then the onion was carefully rolled back again toward Pete's desk where he picked it up again and began picking at it, encouraging it to give off its strong smell. Miss Kitty glared back at him several times and finally said, "Peter, you may stay in at recess."

By recess time it was snowing hard. The children could not go outside to play. They played "Spat-em-out" in the seats and "Aughts-and-crosses" at the blackboards.

By noon, when everyone sat at his desk to eat lunch, the blue coat was forgotten—Bickie hoped it was forgotten. He ate his jam sandwiches with some relish. Still his mind was busy trying to think of some plan for getting rid of the old blue coat. How he wished it had burned up in the fire.

Now if some poor man came along he would give him his coat; or maybe he could lose his coat, but it was so big and bright colored it would be hard to lose in the fields and pastures. If the schoolhouse should bum down maybe the coat would get burned up; or if a flood should swell the creek between school and home maybe he would try to cross it and the coat would be torn off him and lost in the swirling water; or if a tornado came, like the one over by Marshalltown, it could just twist the coat right off his back and carry it way up in the sky and it would never be seen again. Then he could be like the other boys and no one would call him "soldier" any more.

That evening the four boys walked home together, Bickie and Tommie Ross with Pete and Nels Whitney. The snow fall had stopped but a strong wind was blowing. The boys scuffled with one another on the way. The wind lifted Bickie's cap and carried it high in the air.

"It's in those weeds!" Pete shouted. The boys scrambled through the snow drifts; but when they looked the cap was gone. The weed patch covered an acre of ground and the wind blew harder every minute. Bickie put both hands over his ears and ran all the way home.

"Oh, Bickie, where is your cap?" Mother asked when he burst in the door puffing and panting with Tommie just behind him. "Where is your cap?"

"It's lost!" Bickie puffed with a feeling of deep shame. "It's lost, Mother, the wind just pulled it off my head and carried it way up in the air!" He stretched his hands high to show how the wind had carried the cap away. "We hunted everywhere but we couldn't find it. We all looked, didn't we, Tommie?"

Mother looked worried. "You can't go to school without a cap." She put the iron she was using back on the hot kitchen stove and thought for a minute. "I wonder," she said, "I'll look in the big trunk. It may be Grandpa's old plug hat is still in there. It will come down over your ears and shut out the wind. I'm not going to have you getting earache this winter if I can help it."

"Oh, Mother!" Bickie felt a sickness rising in his stomach, "Mother!" he followed her into the small front room of the granary, "Mother, please let me wear a scarf—just wrap my head in a scarf! Please, Mother!"

Mother shook her head and burrowed in the big black trunk. She drew out a big paper sack. "I think it's in here," she exclaimed with relief. She untied the sack and reached in. "Look, it's in fine shape." She drew out the black plug hat. Its crown was stuffed with soft paper. "It's almost new," she said and fitted it on Bickie's head.

Tears stung the boy's eyes. There was a tight, bitter knot in his throat. Then he turned and saw that Tommie had followed them into the room. Tommie was grinning. Bickie gripped him by the shoulder and gave him a hard pinch. Mother took hold of Bickie and turned him around before Tommie could hit him with his doubled fist.

"Bickie," she said, and her voice was low and sad. "I know how hard it is for you to wear the old blue coat and now this plug hat. It is hard to be poor, my boy, but we will not always be so. We will all work together and we will not complain. We will love each other and trust in God. Is that what you want to do?"

Bickie looked down at the floor and nodded his head.

"I can make you a cap, but not before tomorrow morning. I have so much ironing to finish that I will have to work late tonight to get it done." She carried the plug hat out into the kitchen and the boys followed her.

Bickie felt ashamed of himself, but in his mind he could see a picture of himself walking onto the school ground tomorrow morning with the old blue coat and the plug hat. Maybe he could pull the hat off and carry it in his hand when he got near the school. He thought about this for a while and decided that would look even worse.

Chapter 5

The Thunder-Egg Stone

BICKIE AND TOMMIE did the usual chores, bringing in the wood and cobs, carrying water from the pump, feeding the hens and the two calves. Bickie's feet dragged. His heart was too heavy to carry. It was bad enough to go to school with the old blue coat, but to wear the plug hat too…!

"Don't feel bad, Bickie," Tommie whispered as they fetched in the old wash boiler filled with the last load of cobs. "I saw a sack under the coats by the kitchen door. I think its got something in it."

"Sacks usually have something in them," Bickie scoffed. "Was it a paper sack or gunny sack?"

"Come and see."

"It's apples, boys," Mother told them as they started to look for the sack set back under the coats and other garments hanging on the wall by the door. "Red-Hog Smith was here today and he brought us a bushel of apples."

The boys each took an apple and sat down near the stove on the edge of the wood-box.

"I showed Red-Hog the stone you boys dug up and he says it is a thunder-egg. He lifted it and he says it is so heavy it must have a big core of agate inside."

The two boys ran to look again at the big stone propping open the door of the lean-to bedroom.

"Thunder-egg! Thunder-egg!" Bickie said it over and over. What could such a name mean?

"Mother," Tommie called. "Tell us what Red-Hog said about it. Why is it called a thunder-egg?"

"Well, Red-Hog says there are lots of these stones in the California deserts. The Indians call them thundereggs." Mother brushed the curly wisps of black hair from her forehead with her hand and brought another iron from the stove.

"The Indians think the noise of thunder is made by a giant bird. They call it the Thunder-bird. Of course no one ever saw such a bird; but when the Indians found the big egg-like stones in the desert, they supposed they were the eggs of the great Thunder-bird."

Bickie looked at the stone again. He felt strong pride rising in his heart. This wonderful Thunder-egg belonged to him and Tommie. They had found it themselves, dug it up out of the earth.

"How do you s'pose it got here on our land?" Tommie asked. "Was it the flood?"

Mother laughed, "No, I don't think so. I shouldn't wonder if your Uncle Dirk brought it from California. You know he always was collecting stones. There is a pile of stones back by the fence corner in the maple grove. You boys can go and look at them."

Both boys looked out the window. It was getting dark and Bickie decided that he would wait till tomorrow to go and look for Uncle Dirk's pile of stones.

"Mother what did Red-Hog mean when he said it has a core of agate?"

Mother pushed the heavy iron back and forth over the shirt she was ironing. "I think you boys better talk with Red-Hog yourselves. He was in the gold-rush too, you remember. He was in California for several years at the same time your Uncle Dirk was there."

"When can we go?" Bickie asked.

"Of course you couldn't go tonight," she glanced out the window. "It's getting dark already. If you hurry home from school tomorrow afternoon, you may go then."

That night when Bickie lay snuggled under the heavy quilts beside Tommie, he thought about the thunder-egg. He wondered how it happened to be buried in the floor of the cellar. Why didn't Uncle Dirk put it in the pile with the other rocks Mother had told them about. He remembered again that they had never told Mother where they dug up the stone. Again he decided that it didn't matter. After all it was just a stone—a thunder-egg from California, but just a stone after all.

"Tommie," he roused his drowsy brother. "Tommie how do you suppose the thunder-egg came to be buried in our cellar?"

Tommie lifted himself up on his elbow. He rubbed his eyes and yawned. "I still think it was the flood," he said. "Yes, it must have been the flood washed it way over here from California."

"Well, I think Uncle Dirk brought it," Bickie insisted. "Just like Mother told us."

Tommie settled down under the quilts again and said nothing more.

Bickie could not sleep so easily. His thoughts turned to the old blue coat and the plug hat. He twisted and squirmed under the covers as he pictured himself dressed in the hated garments. But when he finally went to sleep he dreamed of the deserts of California strewn with thunder-eggs and enormous birds flying overhead.

When he wakened the following day he couldn't remember for a minute what it was he must be heavy and sad about. Then it rolled over him with a rush. Today he must wear the plug hat—not only the blue soldier coat but the plug hat too.

"Mama, please let me wear just the scarf!" he pleaded. "That will keep my ears warm."

"No, Bickie, I'm afraid of those earaches. The hat will keep out the wind. The scarf isn't thick enough. You must wear the hat and a scarf too."

So Bickie went to school that day swathed to the ears in a pale pink scarf with the plug hat resting firmly on his head. He peered out from under it trying to pick his way among the snow-drifts.

"Oh, look!" His playmates shouted with derision when they saw him. "It's General Snoot!"

"How are you, General Snoot?" they saluted and stood stiffly at attention, mocking him.

In shame and hot anger, Bickie followed the others into the entrance hall at the ringing of the school bell. There he took off his plug hat and hid it with the blue coat and the pink wool scarf under the other wraps. The hat was hard to hide. It was tall and stiff.

The other pupils were already at their desks. He must go in. With one disgusted backward look he entered the schoolroom and tried to forget this newest disgrace in the activities of the morning. He saw Miss Kitty look questioningly at him. She even smiled at him, and his heart warmed for a moment. She couldn't know anything about the torment he was suffering, of course not.

At recess one of the big boys grabbed the hat from its hook before Bickie could reach it. He carried it to the playground. The other boys gathered round.

"Oh, I want to be General Snoot!" one of them cried as he snatched the hat away and put it on his own head.

"No, I'm General Snoot! " another of his mates screamed, grabbing the hat. Bickie looked on in painful embarrassment as the boys scuffled. He secretly hoped the hat would be ruined so it could never be worn again yet he was afraid of what Mother would say, for the hat had been her father's.

Now Nels Whitney came with a long stick. He hoisted the hat on the stick and all the boys fell into parade formation behind the leader as they saluted "General Snoot."

They carried the hat out into a patch of tall weeds where a large road sign stood. It said in big letters:

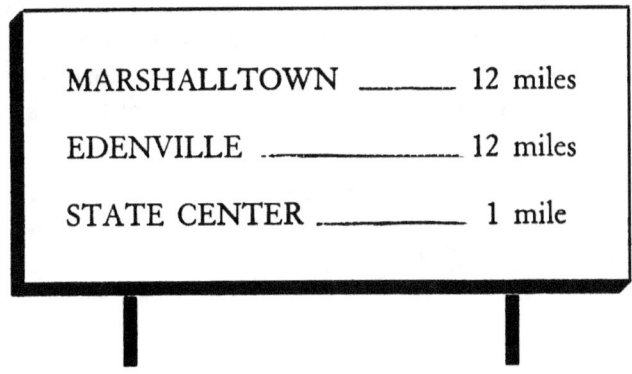

MARSHALLTOWN _____ 12 miles

EDENVILLE _____ 12 miles

STATE CENTER _____ 1 mile

Nels lifted the hat on the end of the stick until he could hook it on the corner of the big sign board.

"Now General Snoot can see which way to go." The boys shouted and danced with mischief. The school bell rang. All the youngsters scrambled for the door. Bickie looked up at the hat high on the sign board. Nels had taken the stick with him. There was no way to get the plug hat down. Miss Kitty would scold if he was late at his desk. Plenty of time to get the hat at noon...he hurried inside.

At noon the hat was gone. The wind could have blown it away or some passer-by could have taken it. The children were all sorry for its disappearance. Surely none of them intended to destroy it. Yet with all their searching it could not be found. That evening Bickie went home with his head wrapped in the pink scarf.

When Mother heard the whole story, she got out some old pieces of wool from one of the trunks. By the light of her coal-oil lamp she worked late into the night. In the morning Bickie had a fine new cap to wear. He never found the old plug hat.

The next morning Pete Whitney waited for Bickie in the weed patch where his other cap had been lost. Pete was a chunky fellow with sandy hair and innocent grey eyes. He didn't laugh a lot or make jokes like his brother Nels, but he could think up more mischief than any of the four boys.

"Come on in here!" He called to Bickie as the Ross boys came along the road. "We'll hide here until we see Miss Kitty come out with the bell. Then we'll run as fast as we can."

Bickie knew why Pete had waited for him. He wanted to fix it so the boys wouldn't have time to make fun of the old blue coat.

"Let's go rabbit hunting tomorrow," Pete whispered as the two boys, breathless from their short run, hung their wraps in the entry hall. "I'll bring Dad's musket and you bring your Dad's—your mother will let you take it, won't she?" Bickie nodded.

"We can go right after school," Pete whispered as they walked into the school room.

Now Bickie had two things to look forward to and think about. Tonight, after school, they would go to ask Red-Hog Smith about the thunder-egg. Tomorrow night they would go rabbit hunting.

The day was not so hard as usual although Miss Kitty was cross and the children had not forgotten their nicknames for him, "Soldier" and "General Snoot."

Bickie was glad when school was dismissed. He and Tommie hurried home and did their chores in a hurry. Then they ran down the road toward Red-Hog Smith's farm.

When the boys found Red-Hog he was just swilling the pigs. The troughs surrounded by the splendid red hogs made a fine sight. They knew that no finer hogs existed in Iowa. They knew that Red-Hog had gotten his name because of his beautiful hogs.

"Did you see our thunder-egg?" Bickie asked the big farmer.

"Yes, I saw it yesterday." Red-Hog smiled at them. "It's a fine stone. Must be one your uncle brought from California."

"I'm sure it is a thunder-egg," he told them. "I lifted it. You can always tell a thunder-egg because it's heavy. Geodes are shaped like eggs too, but they are hollow in the center. You can tell the difference between them by lifting."

"Our stone is awful heavy," Tommie said. "Since John whitewashed it we keep it against our bedroom door just like the stone in your house."

Red-Hog laughed. "The inside of a thunder-egg is of agate—like your marbles, you know." He chewed on his cud of tobacco. "If you saw a thunder-egg in two and polish the halves they look like precious stones. The agate inside is hard and heavy."

"I don't see why Uncle Dirk would want to carry a heavy thing like that all the way from California," Bickie said.

"Your Uncle Dirk liked rocks." Red-Hog dumped the last bucket of swill in the pig's trough and turned toward the house. "I like them too. I brought one home with me. Want to see it?"

The boys stood outside the door on the porch while Red-Hog went in and brought out half of an egg-shaped stone not quite so big as theirs. He held the cut face of it up for the boys to see. It was slick like glass and showed a beautiful picture in colors.

In the center was something that looked like a white throne with a green figure sitting on it. Behind this figure were winged forms like angels in the background. At the foot of the throne flowed a green river, swirling away on either side. The boys looked at the stone overcome with wonder.

"It is the picture of our Lord on His throne in heaven," Red-Hog told them. "Not all thunder-eggs have pictures in them, but the polished stone is always beautiful. Sometimes there are trees and animals."

"Do you suppose our thunder-egg has a picture in it?" Bickie was so full of excitement he could hardly keep from dancing.

"I hefted it when I was over at your place," Red-Hog smiled at them. "I think it must have something pretty inside of it; but the stone is hard to cut and difficult to polish. I had mine done in Marshalltown and the man who did it charged me three dollars and he kept the other half of the stone too."

The boys still gazed at the shining surface of the wonderful stone. Red-Hog let them hold it and they passed their fingers over the slick face of it.

"Where did you fellows find the stone you've got?" Red-Hog asked them.

"We found it buried right in the middle of our cellar. You know the cellar under the house that burned down."

"I guess the flood must have washed it over here from California and buried it here," Tommie said with a wise look.

"No, I don't think so." Red-Hog drew his face into a frown. There were deep wrinkles between his eyes and his mouth was tight and straight. "No, boys, I never seen no stones like this in these parts—I mean I never saw one lying about loose. Someone must have buried it in your cellar," he still frowned and pulled at his heavy beard. "You know I think that must be one of your Uncle Dirk's little jokes. I think he must have brought the stone from California and hid it there."

"Why would he want to bury it?" Bickie asked.

"Oh, I don't know." Red-Hog's face loosened up and he smiled again. "Your Uncle Dirk was like that. He liked queer things. He liked to play tricks on people. He liked stones too. He had a whole collection of them in California. He must have fetched some of them along home with him."

That evening Bickie and Tommie went to the fence corner to see the pile of rocks that Uncle Dirk had collected, but none of them were like the thunder-egg and none of them looked at all pretty. They hurried into the house and told mother about the polished stone Red-Hog had shown them. Then they ran to get the chores done before dark. That night they sat on the floor with the Thunder-egg between them. They talked over all the things Red-Hog had told them and most of all they figured on how they might earn three dollars, so they

Bickie's Thunder Egg

could take their stone to Marshalltown and have it cut
and polished like Red-Hog's.

Chapter 6

The Strange Soldier

THE NEXT MORNING Bickie and Pete brought the muskets along and put them in the weed patch. After the other children and the teacher left the schoolhouse, after school, they brought them out and the four boys went hunting. The guns were loaded with number six shot for squirrels and rabbits.

Before many minutes they startled a rabbit in an adjoining pasture.

"Now get your eyes on the rabbit and shut them tight when you shoot," Bickie warned Pete, steadying his own gun on his shoulder. The rabbit had found temporary shelter in a shallow hole a few yards away.

Bickie lifted his musket and pulled the trigger. In spite of closing his eyes the flash burned his face smartly. He couldn't see anything for a few seconds. The recoil of the heavy gun, although loaded with the lightest of charges, struck Bickie in the chest like a battering ram. Pete was knocked over by the kick-back from his musket. By the time the boys recovered themselves the rabbit had disappeared.

"Better luck next time!" a deep voice spoke from right behind them. "Here, let me help load your guns."

The boys looked around in fear and surprise, but the man appeared quite harmless standing there in the pasture with his worn coat and black slouch hat. Then Bickie saw the G.A.R. badge on his shoulder. All the boys knew what it meant. Nels and Pete's father wore one too. The man was a soldier. They stared at him and none of the four spoke.

"Come, let's get these guns loaded and we'll see if we can't bag something before dark." The stranger spoke in a deep full voice, "We'd better hurry. It will soon be sundown."

Then Nels spoke up, "Where do you live, Mister...?"

Nels was the oldest of the boys and the most talkative. "Did you come from Marshalltown?"

"As a matter of fact I did come from Marshalltown just now," the man smiled down at them. "But it isn't my home. I live in Illinois. I'm here on business. You may call me Rudolph." The man took off his black slouch hat. His hair was thick and curly. His blue eyes twinkled. His moustache and full beard were dark and curly like his hair.

The boys handed their muskets toward the friendly stranger. He took Bickie's first. "Your father must have been a Union soldier," he said, looking at the old blue coat.

Bickie felt his checks grow hot. "My father was captured at Bentonville and he was in Andersonville prison—my Uncle Dirk died before Vicksburg." He used the words exactly as Mother always did.

"Our Daddy came home from war and he was sick—he was sick for a long time and then he died," Tommie informed the man.

"Our Dad was in the cavalry," Nels spoke up, full of pride. "And he isn't sick—he's home."

"Shall we load for geese?" their new friend asked.

"Oh, Mister, that would be fine!" They all agreed.

Rudolph took Bickie's powder flask and poured two measures of powder in the muzzle of the gun. Then he pulled the ramrod from under the barrel of the old musket.

"Have you got some paper?" he asked the boys.

Nels pulled a wad of rough tablet paper out of his pocket. The soldier rammed it down against the powder. Then he took a measure of lead from the flask, poured it in over the powder and rammed another wad of paper down on top of it.

Then the soldier carefully put the ramrod back in its place under the musket barrel and fitted the percussion cap on the hollow tube leading to the powder charge. When the trigger was pulled it would strike the cap, explode it and send a flame down the tube to ignite the powder. Rudolph loaded both muskets, but he gave Pete's back to him to carry. He lifted Bickie's gun to his shoulder and they walked toward the creek.

The sun was already low in the west and the reddish glow that hung over the white snow made it look colder.

Flocks of geese, headed south, flew in great wedges over the farm lands. Most of them flew so high that there was no chance of winging one of them; but, as though some breath of happy fortune attended the new friend they had just made, a flock of geese came swooping down toward the creek that flowed between the school grounds and the Ross farm.

The big birds were coming down for water. Rudolph picked a goose that was sailing in low over the trees and with a terrific burst of noise the old musket blazed out in the quiet evening.

"You got him! You got him! " All the boys shouted as they ran to the spot where the goose lay, just at the edge of the water. He was a fine big fellow.

"Must weigh twelve pounds at least," Rudolph said as he lifted the bird.

He handed it to Bickie. "It's yours, son," he laughed. "It was your musket that shot him. So it's your goose!"

Bickie held out his hands to take the goose with such admiration and excitement filling him—he felt ready to burst with the joy and surprise. What would Mother say when she saw this goose coming in the door? For days they had eaten cornmeal mush for breakfast and for supper and carried jam sandwiches for lunch. Bickie and Tommie felt hungry all the time.

"Maybe you could come home with us." Bickie tightened his hold on the goose. "I know Mother would like to see you."

"Is that your house over there?" The soldier pointed to the unpainted granary.

"Yes, that's our house. It's very near," Bickie urged.

"I would like to come," Rudolph said, patting Bickie's head through the wool cap. "But I'll have to hurry back to town. I'll be around here a few days. I'll see you boys again."

Then a bright idea flashed across Bickie's mind. He looked at the soldier's thin coat. "Maybe you'd like to have my coat," he said. It was right that he should do something for this man who had been so kind. "I really don't need it at all and I think it will fit you—you're a soldier."

Rudolph turned his keen blue eyes on Bickie and looked at him for a minute. "Are you sure you don't need it?" he asked.

"Oh, I have other coats," Bickie boasted. It was true. Tommie was wearing one of them right now and another very ragged one was in the barn. One of the hens had been using it for a nest for months. Yes, Bickie reasoned to himself, he could do without the blue coat very nicely, especially when the man had given them the fine goose.

Rudolph stood for a long time without saying anything. He looked Bickie over and with his sharp eyes measured the coat from tails to collar. Then with a look of sadness in his eyes he said, "All right, little man, I'll take your coat if your mother is willing; but we must walk to the door now and ask her. I don't want you to give away something your mother will be sorry about."

At the door of the granary the boys shouted, "Oh, Mother, look! The soldier man shot the goose for us! Can you cook it now! He is a good soldier!"

Then before Mother could put her iron on the stove or say anything, Bickie said, "May I give him my old blue coat, Mother. It will just fit him and he needs it."

Mother looked at the goose in Bickie's arms. She looked at the other boys, for Pete and Nels came crowding into the kitchen too. Then she looked right over their heads straight at the soldier, Rudolph. Bickie knew that she could see right away how much he needed the coat. She could see that he was cold and his own coat was so thin. Bickie knew that she could see.

"The man's name is Rudolph," Tommie put in. "He shot the goose with our gun."

The soldier had not spoken. He stood there in the door with his hat in his hand smiling.

"If Bickie wants you to have his coat, I think you should take it," Mother said. "Won't you stay and have supper with us? You have made my boys very happy."

"I can't stay this time," the soldier said, smiling still and putting on the old blue coat. "But I will come back again." He stepped out into the snowy evening. The door closed after him.

Then Nels and Pete wanted to lift the goose and there was a great deal of excited chatter. Then the Whitney boys left for home.

Bickie's heart sang. He could not tell whether he was more glad of the goose or of the old blue coat being gone. Such a double blessing was almost more than he could take in.

"Well, well," Mother said, taking the goose in her hands again. "This is wonderful!"

She looked at the old Seth Thomas clock. "It's too late to cook it tonight, but I can dress it and have it ready for tomorrow."

"Let's have our mush and milk right now," Bickie said. "I can't wait. I'm too hungry. The goose can be cooked for us when we come home from school tomorrow."

"That's the best idea," Mother said. "I think John will be back from Marshalltown. He is going to stay home now for a while. That corn should have been picked before the snow." Bickie thought Mother's eyes looked worried, but she brightened at once. "See, I baked fresh bread today, so you can have some bread and jelly and I churned today, too, so there is fresh butter for the bread."

The hungry boys sat down to the scanty supper and ate heartily while Mother filled the big wash boiler with water and put it over the fire as she prepared to dress the goose.

"I think it was good of you to give the soldier your coat," Mother said to Bickie. "He looked so cold, poor fellow. Now I just wonder what you can wear to school."

"I can wear the coat that's out in the barn." Bickie ate his mush in great contentment.

"You mean that one the hen uses for a nest?" Mother laughed. "It's so ragged it wouldn't keep you warm at all." The smile faded from her face and she looked troubled; but she didn't say that Bickie shouldn't have given the coat away. Mother was always quick to pity people who didn't have clothing or food.

"I know what we'll do." Her face brightened, "We'll let you wear my old black coat tomorrow and then I'll see what I can do about fixing you a proper coat of some kind."

Suddenly the mush in Bickie's bowl tasted bitter—the milk must be sour. His stomach didn't feel good either. The old weight pressed down on him just as it had before Rudolph came along this afternoon.

Chapter 7

Bickie's New Coat

MOTHER BUILT up a huge fire under the boiler, while the boys sat at the table over their mush and milk. Bickie wasn't thinking of the goose any more. He was thinking about the black coat.

He knew that Mother had no way of making him a coat or getting him one between now and school time tomorrow morning; but his heart sank lower and lower, down, down into his shoes. Mother's old black coat was cut very full in the back to make room for a bustle. It was rather short on her, but it would be long enough for Bickie—oh, yes, it would be long enough!

"Don't feel so bad about it, Bickie." Mother came over and stood by his chair. She patted his head. "It will only be for a few days and it will keep you warm." She gathered the boy into her arms and sat down in the rocking chair by the stove. Bickie felt something warm and wet on his face—a tear?—Mother crying?

Then Bickie knew that he would wear the old black coat with the bustle back and not complain, for Mother loved him and was trying to do the best thing about the coat. After all she hadn't expected him to give the soldier his old blue coat. Then, there was the goose to think about. His mouth watered and his throat ached with pleasure at the thought of how the roast goose would taste after school tomorrow. He could look forward to that all day, no matter how hard things might be.

When Bickie walked onto the school ground the next morning wearing the black coat with the bustle-back, there were shouts of derisive laughter and a new name was coined.

"Grandma Lucy! Grandma Lucy!" the children shouted in a frenzy of glee and mischief. "Grandma Lucy! Grandma Lucy!Dear Grandma Lucy!"

Bickie set his eyes straight ahead on the schoolhouse steps and marched up them without looking to the right hand or the left. He took off the hateful coat and hung it with the others in the entry way. Now he would be called "Grandma Lucy" all the time. This was worse than "Soldier" or even "General Snoot." At least they were men's names. Overwhelmed with humiliation he went to his desk.

When the spelling class was called, Bickie stood next to Pete Whitney who occupied his usual post at the foot of the class. The first word was "owl" and one by one the whole class missed it, even Bickie.

"Now, Peter," the teacher said, kindly. "Here is a word the whole class has missed. You know how to spell it. I drilled you on it yesterday and you spelled it right for me ten times. Now spell 'owl.'"

Pete's eyes lit up with savage joy, "O–U–L" he spelled in a loud voice. "Hurrah for me! I got a head-mark!"

He started for the head of the class but Miss Kitty met him halfway to his goal and laying a firm hand on his shoulder she gave him a jerk and a shake. "You, little fool!" she cried. "You spelled it wrong! Go back where you belong!"

Bickie shrank with shame over his friend's mistake; but he had little time to be sorry for Pete.

"Spell 'deuce'!" the teacher shouted at him.

The lad stood petrified.

"Spell 'deuce'!" Miss Kitty took a step closer.

Still Bickie couldn't collect his wits or even imagine how to spell 'deuce.'

The teacher came a step closer and raised her hand. Bickie dodged the slap, jerking violently to the left. The line of spellers went over like a row of dominoes set on end.

"Bicknall Haverhill Ross!" the teacher called over the din of confusion. "You may stay in at recess. I will settle with you! The class is dismissed!"

Bickie sat in his seat all through recess with anger in his heart. He would get even with Miss Kitty. He and Pete would think of some good way to get even. But Miss Kitty's sudden anger had cooled and she spent the recess period writing a letter. When the bell rang to close the recess period and the other children marched into the room, Pete whispered to Bickie, "Did you eat the goose?"

Then Bickie remembered the roast goose that would be waiting when they got home tonight. How could he have forgotten it? He looked at Tommie shivering under his ragged jacket. Tommie didn't have enough to eat—not really enough. The goose would taste good.

It was at noon when the boys saw the soldier, Rudolph, approaching the school ground.

"It's our soldier!" Bickie shouted and the four boys ran to meet him.

"How was the goose?" He grinned as he looked down at them. He was wearing the blue soldier coat and on him it looked fine. "We haven't eaten it yet," Bickie told him. "We will have it for supper tonight."

The soldier's eyes were looking sharply at the black coat Bickie was wearing. "Is that your other coat, sonny?" he asked in his deep voice.

"This is one of them," Bickie confessed. Somehow he knew that Rudolph understood about the old blue coat and even about this black one with the bustle-back. He looked straight into the soldier's smiling eyes and he didn't feel ashamed or embarrassed.

"Did you boys ever see a house with a rose vine climbing over the porch and two little green windows up under the gables?" The man asked the question without looking away and with the same warm smile on his face.

"My grandma used to have a house with a rose vine over the porch," Nels said. "It was a red rose vine, too, but she doesn't live there any more. She lives with us."

"Does the house have two little windows up under the gables?" the man asked.

"I don't think so." Nels scratched his yellow hair along his neck under his cap. "Does the house have to have little green windows? "

"The house I'm looking for must have two little green windows up under the gables," Rudolph said.

"Why do you want to find it?" Bickie said. "Do you want to live there?"

"No," he said with a look of sadness creeping into his eyes. "No, a solder friend of mine used to live there, but he was killed in the war. He told me about his house and I want to see it."

The boys looked at one another. They liked Rudolph. He had shot the goose for them and he spoke kindly to them almost as if they were grown men. They would be glad to help him find the house with the rose vine over the front porch, but it was wintertime now and none of them could remember which houses had rose vines until springtime should come and the roses bloom again.

The sharp clang of the school bell drew them back to the schoolhouse door. Bickie turned at the entrance to wave at Rudolph. He still stood at the edge of the playground with his black slouch hat in his hand. Now he raised it and with an elegant gesture swept the old hat low toward the ground, then high over his head.

"Maybe he'll be waiting for us when last recess comes," Pete whispered to Bickie, but when recess came there was no soldier lingering about the Ferguson school.

It was getting close to four o'clock and Bickie began to think more and more about the goose. How near would they have to come to the door of home to smell the goose? Would Mother have gotten an onion and maybe a few potatoes to cook with it? Would she have it stuffed with dressing?

Bickie sat at his desk thinking so hard about the goose that he forgot where he was. His mind wandered in far off places where roast goose and mashed potatoes and pumpkin pie and other luxuries abounded on every side.

He was awakened from his daydream by a sharp voice from the front of the room.

"Bicknall, open your book. Stop your daydreaming! and get to work or I shall have you come to the front of the room."

Bickie hurried and got out his Steele's Physiology. He was not willing to take any chances on having to go to the front of the room. There he would have to stand in a corner with his face to the wall and a book in his hand. If he so much as moved a foot or a hand there would be a smart cuff on the ear. He bent over the Steele's Physiology, determined to master his lesson.

The colored picture at the beginning of the lesson chapter drew Bickie's interest. Underneath it there were words written. He spelled them out. They said, "alimentary canal." Now Bickie had no idea what kind of canal that might be, but clearly the picture was of a human being. He knew that these things pictured in color on the figure were the insides of people—their stomachs and intestines, their lungs, liver and brain. He wondered if Miss Kitty looked like that on the inside. Very likely she did. A bright idea came into his head. He drew out a sheet of drawing paper from his desk.

With care and considerable skill he copied the figure on the page, but he gave it features with a proper head and a top-knot. Then he sketched in the lungs, liver, stomach, intestines and all the other colored things in the picture, making them as faithful to detail as possible. It took a long time. When the drawing was done he felt proud of it. He would show it to Tommie, to Pete and Nels. He wrote in big letters at the top of the sheet, "MISS KITTY."

Chapter 8

A Rush Corn Husking

BICKIE LOOKED DOWN at the finished picture on his desk. He was just reaching his foot across the aisle to nudge Pete's shoe when he realized that Miss Kitty was standing right behind him. Then he felt a pair of strong fingers fasten onto his arm. It was such a hard pinch, Bickie felt sure a piece of flesh would be pulled right out of his arm; but at last the teacher let go.

Tears stung Bickie's eyes, but he would not cry. He did not make a sound. He held onto his arm, for it ached more than anything! He pushed the picture into his desk and laid his head on his hands.

He was roused from his sorrow by a poke in the foot and Pete pressed a note across the narrow space between their desks.

"Don't fel bad. I no hou to fix er."

It was signed, "P–e–t–e."

Then it was time to go home. The order was given to put away books and march out. Bickie took down his despised black coat, waited till most of the children had gone, then he walked home with Tommie and the Whitney boys.

Their talk was about the soldier who had come again that day.

"Mother says he is a good man," Tommie said. "She says he has kind eyes."

"I wonder why he wants to see the house where his friend lived. If the soldier is already dead in the war, why does he want to see his house?" Nels spoke his question out to the other boys.

"Maybe he wants to buy the house," Bickie said.

"I don't think he's got any money to buy houses," Pete answered. "His clothes are shabby and thin and he looks hungry."

"He looks clean, though," Bickie defended Rudolph. "Even though his clothes are ragged they are clean. Mother says you can always tell a gentleman even if his shirts are ragged."

"When he comes back next time, we'll ask him more about the house. I just bet we could find it. Isn't it funny his friend didn't tell him where to look for it?" Nels questioned.

They had come to the gate of the Ross farmyard. Bickie and Tommie went in walking backward and swinging their dinnerpails, waving and shouting to Pete and Nels as they went on toward their place farther up the road.

On the front steps the boys paused for just a minute. They sniffed the air. They could catch the fragrance of roast goose. They threw open the door and walked into the delicious perfume.

The table was set. Mother had put on her best tablecloth and there was the bread she had baked yesterday with a pot of wild strawberry jam. On the warming oven of the range the big platter stood ready for the roast goose. The delightful smells that filled the little house made Bickie a little dizzy. Mother came in with such a face of tenderness, both the boys threw their arms around her.

"Is the goose done?"

"Did you make dressing?"

"Is that onion I smell?"

Mother laughed and her black eyes sparkled. "Hurry now, she said. "Get in the wood and cobs before dark. Get the chores done and then when John gets in we will all be ready to eat."

The chores were never done with more cheerfulness or with greater haste. John came in from the barn and the family gathered round the table bowing reverently while Mother said grace.

The goose was a magnificent bird. From some unknown place Mother had gathered the material to make a fine stuffing. There were roasted potatoes in the pan too, and baked apples came from the warming oven. A pitcher of milk from the cold cupboard in the shed made the meal perfect.

"Where did you get the potatoes?" John asked as he filled his plate.

"Red-Hog Smith came by and dropped off a bushel for us," Mother said.

"Why would he do that?" John wondered.

"He said someone in State Center gave him fifty cents and told him to leave us a bushel of his best potatoes. Who do you suppose it was, John?"

John wrinkled his face as much as he could with the tremendous job he was doing on the goose. "I can't think who that might be," he said.

"There are so many kind people in the world," Mother looked round on the three boys with her laughing eyes. "Next year we will have our own potatoes."

"Yes, I wish we could save this bushel for seed." John made a wry face. "I never tasted such good potatoes."

They all knew why there had been no potato patch this last year. It was because of Daddy's illness and all the money they had to spend for his medicine and doctors and the funeral. They were lucky, as John said to get seed corn and lucky to get the twenty acres planted. It was ready to husk now. In fact it should have been husked before the October snowstorm, but that was pretty well gone, now. John would begin husking tomorrow. Bickie thought about all these things as he soberly stuffed himself with the roast goose.

Then he realized that Mother was talking again. Bickie's mind came back to the table and the good supper.

"Red-Hog said the man who gave him the fifty cents for the potatoes was someone he had never seen before."

All at once Bickie remembered the look in Rudolph's eyes when he asked him about the black coat. He felt almost sure that Rudolph must have been the one who sent the potatoes. But he didn't say anything to Mother.

The next morning while Bickie and Tommie were dressing they heard a rough voice in the kitchen. Bickie peeked out the open door. It was Hake Collins.

"I see your corn is ready to husk." Hake was saying to Mother and John. "Now I intend to perteck my rights. I'm puttin four men into that field of your'n the first of the week and their wages will come out of the price of the corn when it's sold."

"You don't need to do that, Mr. Collins," John spoke calmy. "I will get the corn husked and marketed and you will be repaid the entire amount that it brings."

"Well, I don't trust ye, John." Hake chewed on his cud of tobacco. "I been awful good to you folk. Then you go and let the house burn down. I don't trust ye with that corn."

"But, Mr. Collins, the wages of four men to pick that corn will be fifty dollars or more!"

"Reckon as how it will, Mizz Ross." Hake spat a mouthful of tobacco juice on the floor. "But as I was say'in I been awful good to you folk and I got to perteck my rights.

The old farmer turned and stepped out into the snowy morning. John and Mother looked at one anther.

"Fifty dollars, John! We can't let him do it! " Mother's face was red and her eyes very bright.

"We won't do it either." John sat up to the table where Mother had already filled the bowls with mush. "We will pick it ourselves, we will. Even if we have to hang a lantern on the buck-board of that wagon, we'll get that corn in this week!"

"Bick and Tom," John turned to the boys, "You fellows don't get to go to school this day or any more days until that corn is in. Do you hear?"

"I'll help too," Mother said. "We'll all work together and we'll work as hard and as fast as we can. We'll fool Hake this time."

As soon as breakfast was over they all went to the corn field. Tommie made a great show of driving the horses, although they were well trained and would stop and start when spoken to and they were accustomed to husking corn.

Mother with John and Bickie twisted off the ears, husking them out as they broke them free and tossed them into the wagon bed.

They worked without talking. Every bit of strength and energy they had they spent on the job before them. At meal time Mother brought food and a hot drink. They worked on till sundown. As they filled the wagon John drove it into the farm yard and shoveled the corn into the back room of the big barn which was used for a granary now that the real granary had become a house.

By the end of the second day Mother and John both looked distressed. They were not nearly half through and there were only two more days before the Sabbath. None of the Ross family would work on that day. No not even to protect themselves from Hake Collins.

On the third morning Red-Hog Smith drove into the yard. "I see you folk are husking your corn," he said. "I'll give you a hand today and tomorrow and John can help me back a couple days when I start on my field."

They looked at Red-Hog with unbelieving eyes. "God must have sent you!" Mother said and Bickie saw tears on her cheeks.

Red-Hog Smith was the best corn-picker in the country. There was no question now. They would finish on time.

Still Bickie trudged along through the rows of corn, doing his best to keep up with John and Mother while Red-Hog drove his own wagon along at the other end of the field.

Bickie's shoes, which had been worn and thin at the first of the week were now completely broken. His bare toes, red and frostbitten peeked out of the ragged holes in the shoes.

"That boy ought to have a new pair of shoes," Red-Hog Smith remarked to John as they were shoveling in the last of the corn.

"Corn's all mortgaged to Hake Collins, you know," John said. "How can we buy shoes?"

"Look here, John," Red-Hog said. "There is about enough corn left in my wagon to make the price of a pair of shoes. Jump in, Bickie. I'll tend to this myself. It won't be you and it won't be your mother."

Bickie, with a boost from John, was pushed aboard Red-Hog's wagon and they drove into State Center, where the corn was exchanged for a sturdy pair of shoes.

Bickie's heart swelled with pride, not only because of the new shoes, but because a fine big strong man like Red-Hog Smith had taken him into the shoe shop and called him "son" and made him try on pair after pair of shoes until the very best ones were found. It was almost like having a father.

When Red-Hog drove home he let Bickie out at the gate and he ran into the house eager to tell Mother and show her the new shoes.

"I'm afraid it isn't right," she said to John. "Of course he did need the shoes, but the corn was mortgaged."

Then John's face darkened. "Mother, Hake Collins doesn't know the difference between blood and money!" He brought his hard fist down on the table top. "I don't want you to speak to me about this—ever again!" And Mother never did.

When the corn was sold it didn't bring quite a hundred dollars. When Hake came over on Monday morning to start his men on the corn field, John met him at the gate with the money in his hand. The elevator man from State Center had come out Saturday night and paid cash for it.

Bickie stood close to John, proud that he, too, had helped gather in the crop and save the extra fifty dollars.

Hake Collins counted the money twice. Then he climbed back into his wagon. He leaned over the side, whip in hand, "Mind ye, there's another two hundred and four dollars and three cents that has got to be in by New Years or else out ye go!"

When Hake came over on Monday morning, John met him at
the gate with the money.

Chapter 9

Hake Takes the Thunder-Egg

JOHN DID NOT ANSWER HAKE. He stood scowling at the old farmer as he drove out of the barnyard and down the road. Then he turned back toward the granary house where Mother watched from the kitchen window.

"Oh, John," she said as they went in, I hope you didn't make him angry! "

"I didn't speak to him. Did I, Bick?" John took off his cap and sat down at the breakfast table.

"John just gave him the money and he counted it and counted it," Bickie told Mother. "But he didn't say any thing, John didn't."

Bickie and Tommie gulped their mush and hurried off to school. They had missed four days. Practicing for the Thanksgiving program had begun last week. Bickie knew they must have missed important things. But one special thing happened that day. The soldier, Rudolph, came for another visit. He walked onto the playground at the last recess.

"Are you sure you don't know anything about that house?" he asked them when they ran to meet him. "Remember I asked you about a house. It had a rose vine—a yellow rose vine...."

Then something seemed to open in Bickie's mind. He looked at Tommie in amazement. "Why—why—Tommie! The house that burned!—It had a yellow rose vine and two little windows—green ones—!"

He turned to face Rudolph. "Maybe you're looking for the house we used to live in. That house is all burned up now, but it did look like you say. I never thought of it the other time you asked."

Then Rudolph took Bickie by the hand and drew him close to his side. "I rather think I am looking for that very house. Of course, as you say, it's all burned up now; but I would like to see the place where it stood. You tell your mother that tomorrow evening I will come and talk with her about it."

"Yes, sir, Bickie said and stood looking up at the soldier.

"I am an army chaplain," Rudolph explained to the boys. "I was with the forty-second Illinois regiment. Do you know what a chaplain is?"

None of the boys knew.

"A chaplain is a sort of preacher or minister who goes along with the army. He holds services for the soldiers. If they are sick he visits them. He reads the Bible to the ones who have time to listen and many times the soldiers tell him their troubles and their secrets."

The school bell clanged and the boys hurried into the schoolroom. Bickie thought over what Rudolph had said.

When the Ross boys went home that evening they were full of excitement, "Mother, Mother!" Bickie burst into the kitchen ahead of Tommie. "Our soldier is coming—the one who shot the goose for us. He is coming to talk with you this evening."

"Well, that's nice," she said.

"He wants to talk with you about our house burning up," Tommie added.

"What's this ... ?" John asked, but he was interrupted by a sound of heavy steps outside the door. There was a sharp knock on the door. Mother opened it. Hake Collins stood outside.

He pushed into the room. Mother handed him a chair and motioned for him to sit near the fire for the day was cold. Bickie and Tommie sat in the door of their bedroom with the thunder-egg between them and they listened while Hake Collins told Mother and John that they would have to give him more "security," since the corn had brought such a low price.

"But we don't have anything that is worth much," Mother explained to him. "You see, after the fire, people gave us things. Look around and see if there is anything you think is valuable enough to take as security."

Hake's eyes examined the room. He looked at the stove for a long time. "Perty good stove," he remarked.

"It belongs to Red-Hog Smith," Mother told him. "He loaned it to us."

Bickie saw John's hand clench into a tough, hard fist. "Remember," he spoke and his voice was hard and stem, "Our corn crop was mortgaged to you and our buildings and farm are mortgaged to you; but we ourselves and the beds we sleep in and the table we eat from and the chairs we sit on are not mortgaged to you and there is no paper that says so."

"You needn't get so fussed up, John." Hake looked along his sharp nose like a hunter sighting down a gunbarrel. "I been good to you folks. All I want is to perteck my rights."

Then he noticed the stone between the two boys. He bent forward to stare at it. They were patting and stroking it as they often did when they were dreaming about the time when they would have enough money to take the thunder-egg into Marshalltown and have it polished.

"What kind of stone have you young-uns got?" he asked, getting up from his chair and coming over to kneel by the stone.

"It's a thunder-egg, that's what it is," Tommie piped up in a shrill excited voice. "We're going to take it to Marshalltown and have it cut and polished. It's just like Red-Hog Smith's thunder-egg."

Hake picked up the stone and looked at it. "A thunderegg, huh?" He shifted the weight of the stone from one hand to the other. "I seen that thunder-egg of Red-Hog's, right perty it is, too."

He turned the stone over and examined it from every side. Bickie felt a strange fear rising in his chest. He reached for the stone, but Hake stepped back. "Costs money to have stones cut and polished," he laughed a thin crackling laugh. "Reckon it'll be a long time fore you young-uns have enough to do that, eh?"

"It'll keep." Bickie still held his hands out for the stone. "It won't spoil. Even if we have to wait till we're grown up, we'll wait. Won't we, Tommie?" "No, I hain't goin to give it to ye." Hake looked at the two boys. "I'll tell ye what I'm goin to do. I'll just take this here stone. I know as how it came from California. It may have something perty inside it like Red-Hog Smith's stone and then again it mayn't." He laughed again. "I'll just take it as—a—sort of interest. It ain't much account of course, but I like perty things."

Bickie's heart leaped into his throat. "No, no!" he tried to take the thunder-egg from Hake, but the old farmer, still cackling his thin laugh, balanced the stone in one hand while he put on his fur cap with the other.

"It's only a stone, Bick," John said in a low voice. "If Hake has sunk so low that he even robs children of their toys, I guess there isn't anything to do about it."

Mother started to speak, but John silenced her with a wave of his hand and without another word Hake Collins walked out into the November evening with the thunder-egg.

"Now you boys hurry and get the chores done. See it's dark already!" Mother said. "Don't feel bad about your stone. Next summer you can dig up a lot more. I'm sure there are plenty more as good as that one."

"But not from California, Mother! Not from California! Not thunder-eggs!" Bickie's voice had risen to a wail. He was very near crying. He grabbed the cob baskets and the old boiler they used for cobs and started for the barn with Tommie at his heels.

"Let's not even think about that mean old Hake," Tommie said in a trembling voice. "Let's think about tomorrow night when Rudolph comes."

"I wonder why he wants to talk about our burned house." Bickie swiped his mittened hand over his eyes and nose to brush away the tears he couldn't keep back.

"I know what! Let's tell him about the thunder-egg. Maybe he could help us get it back. I think Hake might be scared of Rudolph—he's a soldier, you know."

After supper was over and the boys tucked in bed, Bickie could not sleep. He kept thinking of Hake and the thunder-egg. Now Hake would take the stone to Marshalltown and have it polished and they would never see the beautiful thing inside it. The more he thought about it the heavier his heart grew. He finally sat up in bed to ease the weight of it a little.

He thought of how long ago they had found the stone. It must be at least five months since they dug it out of the cellar floor. It was just a stone—just a stone, but Bickie hadn't realized how much he cared for it until now, after Hake Collins had carried it away.

Chapter 10

Soldier Rudolph Visits

THE FOLLOWING MORNING when Bickie and Tommie walked into the schoolroom, Miss Kitty looked up from her desk, "Come here, Bicknall. I have something to say to YOU."

Bickie dragged his feet to the teacher's desk.

"I have been thinking about who should recite the poem in our Thanksgiving play. I think you could do it very well. Would you like to?"

Bickie looked at Miss Kitty. She had the same thin face, the same grey top-knot and the flat bow of black ribbon against her throat. He remembered why she was so skinny—no onions—and a flush of shame spread over his face. She looked beautiful to him in that instant. He saw for the first time that her eyes were blue and at this moment, very kind. "I would like it," he said, scuffing the toe of his new shoe on the rough floor.

"Then here it is," she gave him the handwritten poem. "Learn it as fast as you can. The small children are going to act out the coming of the Mayflower and the landing on Plymouth Rock. You will say the verses while the pantomine is going on. I think it will be very nice."

Bickie could not speak another word. He took the paper from the teacher's hand and stumbled back to his desk.

"Now what have you got to copy?" One of the big boys whispered as he tried to trip Bickie in the aisle.

"What-sha been up to now?" another said as Bickie thrust the sheet of paper in his desk.

He didn't answer them. He knew that his face was fiery red. But his heart was singing. He looked at Miss Kitty and she was smiling. He looked about the school-room, at the old carved and whittled desks, the cracked blackboards, the roguish children and the thin, greyhaired teacher. For the first time they looked pleasant to him.

He had seen the children practicing for the pantomine yesterday. There was a "shore" and a boat fashioned out of cardboard where the children, who represented the Pilgrims, stood on the "Mayflower" and looked out over the "stern and rock-bound coast."

Bickie heard the teacher say that they were going to make big blue waves of paper and they would have Plymouth Rock on the shore surrounded with smaller rocks to look like the "rockbound" coast where the pilgrims landed.

Bickie studied all his lessons that day and he played hard at recess. He couldn't help telling Pete about the wonderful thing that had happened and Pete told all the other boys. For the time being Bickie was an important fellow on the playground, in spite of his bustleback coat. They allowed him to be catcher in the big boy's ball game at noon and when his side came to bat, he hit two home-runs.

Along with all this, Bickie found time to sneak frequent looks at the paper Miss Kitty had given him. By evening he knew the first eight verses. There were twelve altogether.

That night while the boys did their chores Bickie spoke his piece for Tommie and the cows and the hens and the two work horses. Later he even said them for Mother.

Supper was barely cleared away when Rudolph knocked at the door. The boys ran to let him in. "Mrs. Ross," he took off his cap and gave her his coat. "Ever since I came to Marshalltown and State Center, I have been trying to locate a certain house. I had other things to attend to and right after the war I was ill for a long time. So I am very late—three years late in fact, getting to this part of the country. Now I have good reasons to believe that it is your house I have been looking for."

Bickie and Tommie sat in the door of their lean-to bedroom just as they had last evening; but now there was no thunder-egg between them. Bickie remembered and looked at Tommie. He could see that Tommie remembered too.

"The boys told me that you asked them about our house." Mother gave Rudolph a chair near the fire.

"Yes," the soldier hesitated. "I'm sorry to bring up painful memories, but it may be of some importance to you. Did you have a brother with the Union forces whose name was Dirk Himes?"

"Yes, of course!" Mother's eyes flashed and she leaned forward to hear every word the strange soldier might have to say. "Yes, my brother always lived with us. He went to California with the forty-niners. When he came back he brought a little money and he bought this farm and built the house. It is burned now. I guess the boys told you." She looked around the whitewashed walls of the granary kitchen.

"Did your brother ever say anything that might lead you to think he had money or some valuable thing hidden in the house?"

"Yes," Mother pushed the black ringlets from her forehead. "Yes, he did. When he was leaving with my husband to enlist with the other Iowa volunteers, he said, 'Fietta, there's enough money in this house to keep you till we come back. Look for it. I'm sure you'll find it when you need it.' " Then he pointed down at the floor.

"Did you think he meant that some money was hidden?"

"Well, I wasn't sure," Mother said. "He may have meant the money value in the house. He was a great joker—my brother—he always laughed a lot and talked a great deal of nonsense. Often we didn't know whether to take the things he said seriously or as a joke."

"Did you ever look for such a thing?"

"Oh, yes." Mother's eyes darkened with pain. "When my husband was sick for so long and we had so little, I spent a lot of time looking for whatever Dirk had talked about. I looked through all his trunks and clothes. I even pried up a couple boards from the floor. They seemed to be a little loose—but there was nothing. We had to borrow money and mortgage our place."

"Well, Rudolph leaned forward in his chair and looked intently at Mother, "I was with Dirk Himes the last hours of his life. I am an army chaplain. I suppose the boys told you. He had been wounded and he was feverish and delirious most of the time; but once he seemed more calm. He took my hand and pulled me down so I could hear what he wanted to say. He was very weak. He talked very fast and as near as I can remember he said something like this, 'My sister and her young-uns live in Iowa, State Center. You'll know the house—yellow rose vine on porch—little green windows up under gable. Name is Ross—look for the stone—the stone—!' Then I couldn't make out the rest of what he said. He never was able to say anything more."

Mother and John looked at one another in amazement. Bickie and Tommie went to stand beside Rudolph.

"You really knew my Uncle Dirk?" Bickie said. "I was just a little boy when he went away. Tommie wasn't even born yet, but I remember him. He was like Mother."

"Yes, Rudolph smiled at them. "He was very much like your mother, same eyes, same hair, same smile. Of course I didn't know him very well. I only saw him after they called me and told me to go to him because he was going to die." The smile had left the soldier's face and a look of deep sadness replaced it.

Mother and John still looked at each other and Bickie could see that they were perplexed.

"You said—a stone?" John scratched his head and unbuttoned his shirt collar. "I can't understand what that might mean."

"Was any part of the house made of stone?" Rudolph asked John.

"Yes, of course, the cellar walls and the foundations were made of red sandstone. They are still out there under the snow. You can't see them now, but tomorrow we could look them over."

"I'm sure he said, 'the stone.'" Rudolph seemed to be talking more to himself than to John. "It may not mean a thing. He may not even have known what he was saying."

"He was always interested in stones," Mother said. "He liked to collect them even when he was a small boy."

"His mind may have been wandering back to the goldrush days in California." John scratched his head.

"Thanks for coming anyway," Mother spoke kindly. "I think it was a kind thing for you to come here to find us and tell us about this."

"I had other business here in Marshalltown," Rudolph said as he stood up and reached for the old blue soldier's coat and his black hat. "You see the G.A.R. was organized three years ago this winter. One of the important things they do is to look into matters like this that concern the widows and orphans and other relatives of the men who fought for our Union."

"Well, come back tomorrow and we'll have a look around the old foundation." John said as Rudolph went out the door.

"A stone—a stone," Bickie said the words over and over in his mind. There was something in the back of his head and suddenly it burst forth in an excited cry, "The thunder-egg! The thunder-egg!"

He began to dance wildly about the kitchen floor.

Mother grabbed his arm and drew him to her, "What are you saying? What's this about the thunder-egg?"

Bickie broke away from her and threw himself on the floor beside Tommie, "My thunder-egg! my thunder-egg! That's the stone Uncle Dirk meant! I'm sure it is! We found it right there in the cellar floor. I'll bet he put it there! And now Hake Collins has taken it!"

Mother jerked Bickie to his feet. "You never told me you found it in the cellar floor." Mother looked serious "You said you dug it out of the dirt."

"We did, Mother," Tommie put in. "We did! We dug it out of the dirt right in the middle of the old cellar floor. We took up all the boards and leaned them against the sides and then we played Treasure-dig. The stone was right there, so we dug it up."

"Tomorrow you must show us exactly where you found the stone," John said. "This might be important."

"But Hake has the stone!" Bickie almost screamed in his excitement and anger. "Hake has the stone and he will never give it up."

"No, I guess he wouldn't," John said with a shake of his head and banging of his fist on the table.

As Bickie lay in his bed that night he knew that he must find some way to get the thunder-egg back. There must be some way. Maybe there was something valuable inside it. Perhaps it was a special kind of thunder-egg that was worth a lot of money and Uncle Dirk knew it. Maybe Hake Collins knew it too. He collected stones just like Uncle Dirk had. He kept a whole pile of them on his front porch. Of course Hake couldn't know what Rudolph had told them tonight.

Since he found it hard to go to sleep Bickie repeated the verses of his poem over and over until suddenly it was morning.

Chapter 11

The Thunder-Egg Reappears

AS THE BOYS WERE LEAVING for school the following morning, Mother called both of them to her. She put an arm around each, "Now, boys, I don't think you should say anything about Rudolph's visit here last night. I don't think you should mention the thunder-egg or Hake Collins or anything about this affair."

"Can't we tell anyone?" Tommie pouted.

"No," she insisted. "It is much better not to talk about things that are the private business of our family."

At Ferguson School the practice for the coming Thanksgiving program took up most of the time. All the children's talk was about the recitations, the songs and the Thanksgiving play.

The older boys were busy getting ready the things for scenes in the play. The girls were making blue waves from tissue paper. Miss Kitty was trying to fit the small children with suitable costumes, pilgrim costumes.

Bickie knew all of his verses now and when they practiced with him in the background, the older boys and girls sat in the back of the room and clapped their hands in delight. It was a beautiful pantomime and Bickie's voice carried well.

"Now, what shall we use for Plymouth Rock?" Miss Kitty asked the children.

"How big is Plymouth Rock?" the children wanted to know. "Did you ever see it, Teacher?"

"Yes, I saw it once," she said. "It isn't quite as big as my desk—not so high."

"Maybe we could use boxes and cover them with cardboard," one of the big boys suggested.

"That might do." Miss Kitty stepped across the front of the room to measure how much space there would be for the "Rock."

"We could whitewash the cardboard to make it look like snow and ice. I guess it was cold when the Pilgrims landed, wasn't it?" A girl in the back seat made this suggestion.

Then an idea struck Bickie like a hammer in the chest. "We could get some real stones and rocks," he almost shouted the words. "We could pile them around the Plymouth Rock to make it look more natural and hide the edges of the cardboard."

"Why that is an excellent idea!" Miss Kitty smiled at Bickie. Then her face grew thoughtful. "But where would we get the stones in this deep snow. It would be hard to go out looking for them."

Then Bickie spoke out again in a voice that quivered with excitement. "I know that Hake Collins has a pile of stones on his front porch. Of course some of them are valuable stones. But he might be willing to let us have some of them for the program."

The teacher beamed, "Oh, I'm sure Mr. Collins will let us have them. He's treasurer of the School Board and very interested in the program. I will ask him myself."

Bickie could hardly settle himself to study for the rest of the day. Of course Hake Collins might not bring the thunder-egg to the program, even if Miss Kitty asked him for the stones. He might bring some of the others; but probably the thunder-egg was on top of the pile and would be convenient to pick up. Bickie would just have to wait and see. It was hard to wait. But if—IF—IF Hake brought the thunder-egg to the program, then what?

He resolved that if Hake should bring the stone, he, Bickie, would never let him take it away again. After all, Hake had practically stolen it. No one gave it to him. No one said he might have it.

He could hide the thunder-egg; but that wouldn't be exactly honest. Hake had said he was taking it for interest. Bickie didn't know what that meant, but it was probably something important. Of course someone could offer to buy it—maybe Rudolph would; but if Hake found out that anyone was willing to pay money for the stone the price would be very high. Maybe Rudolph didn't have any money either.

Bickie puzzled over the problem all day and Miss Kitty had to speak sharply to him before the last recess.

"Do you suppose Rudolph came today?" Tommie asked Bickie on the way home.

"He said he would come today. Let's run!"

At home John met the boys at the gate. "Come with me," he said in a stern voice, "I want you to show me exactly where you found that stone I whitewashed."

The boys walked with John to the open cellar of the burned house. The snow had been shoveled out of the cellar and thrown up in a great pile at the side. The floor was bare and it was no longer possible to see the hole where the stone was dug up so many months ago.

"Now, show me." John took Bickie's arm.

"I think it was right in the middle of the floor."

"Well, we are sure now that your stone had something valuable in it," John told them. "I don't suppose it matters greatly where you found it. The important thing now is to get it away from Hake Collins."

"How will you do that?" Tommie asked.

"I really don't know," John said. "It's no use to ask him for it. It's no use to try to buy it. The minute some one acts like it's valuable..."

"Hake just wouldn't let them have it at any price," Bickie finished.

"Was Rudolph here?" Bickie asked.

"Yes, he was here. He helped me shovel out this snow. He thinks it wasn't an ordinary stone. He thinks it had something hidden inside it—maybe gold or money. It was awful heavy—remember?"

"Oh, oh!" Both Bickie and Tommie caught their breath with excitement.

"He says that Uncle Dirk said, 'Find the stone.' Well, you boys found the stone—I'm pretty sure you did—and now it's gone!" John looked vexed and angry.

"I should have made Hake give it back to you." He looked at Bickie. "I had no idea it was of any value. I thought he was just trying to be mean."

"Does Rudolph know that Hake took the stone?" Bickie said. "Yes, I told him." John kicked at a scrap of charred shingle in the rubble on the cellar floor.

"Didn't he know what to do?" Tommie asked.

"No, of course not." John was impatient. "He is going to hunt up the man in Marshalltown who cut and polished Red-Hog Smith's stone. It might be that Hake would take the stone in there."

"What if they cut it open and there is lots and lots of money in it?" Tommie danced about in the bare cellar in great glee. "Then we could have jelly every day and potatoes and pumpkin pie and beef stew!"

"Don't be such a dunce!" John picked up the shovels still lying on the cellar floor. "We don't have the thunderegg any more and we don't count our chickens until they're hatched. There isn't much chance of anything hatching for us with Hake sitting on the thunder-egg."

They all laughed at John's joke and felt better. Bickie didn't speak of his plan to get Hake to contribute some stones to the Thanksgiving program. He knew there was only a chance that the thunder-egg might be brought to the schoolhouse and he hadn't figured out any way to keep the stone if it should come within his reach again. It was possible that Hake might already have done something with the stone. Bickie cringed inside at the thought. He doubled his fists as he thought of it and felt that he would be glad to fight Hake Collins and make him give up the stone. He had taken it when it didn't belong to him. He had stolen it. He should be punished like any other thief. Bickie worked himself into a fury of anger over it.

The days passed quickly. There was little news from Rudolph. He had found the stone-cutter in Marshalltown. The man would be watching for the stone to come in and he would notify Rudolph when it did; but Hake might keep the thunder-egg for years before doing anything with it. He probably would. No one seemed to have any definite plan. Even Bickie had not made up his mind what to do.

Finally came the night of the Thanksgiving program. Everyone in the school district was there. The boys had asked Rudolph to come. He promised that he would because Bickie was to give the recitation for the pantomime.

Ferguson Schoolhouse was crowded to the doors when the Rosses got there. Bickie went behind the curtain drawn across the platform. He must see exactly where he would stand for his part in the program.

The pantomime was to come first on the evening's entertainment and the scenery was all in place.

Bickie's heart almost pounded itself out of his chest when he looked down at the "Plymouth Rock" and the other stones around it. They were all neatly white-washed with a bluish tinge in the right places to make them look icy and cold. His eye examined every stone, but the thunder-egg was not among them. He felt a little sick.

There was no time to grieve over the failure of his plan. The program was about to begin and Miss Kitty, looking very nice, came to show him where he must stand.

Bickie spoke out with a strong voice and he remembered every word of his recitation. The pantomime went forward beautifully and when it was ended there was such a burst of hand-clapping that the little schoolroom shook with it. Bickie felt his cheeks grow hot and his head felt light from the excitement.

He stumbled out through the scenery to the rear door and went through it into the big store-room beyond. It was dimly lighted by a single lantern hung from a hook high on the wall. He saw that the lantern wick was turned a little too high and the glass was smoking over. He reached up to turn it lower and stumbled over something on the floor. He looked down, then knelt. His head reeled and he wondered if he had suddenly gone crazy. The thunder-egg lay there against the wall right under the lantern!

Chapter 12

Hake's Mashed Toe

BICKIE LAID HIS HAND on the thunder-egg. It was surely the same stone that Hake Collins had taken from him over two weeks ago. He felt of it and turned it over, his mind a confused whirl of troubled thoughts.

Why was the thunder-egg in this store-room. If Hake brought it for the program, and he must have, why wasn't it on the platform? Who had put it here and why? Most important of all, what could he do with it?

Bickie sat down and took his treasure in his lap. There was ordinarily nothing in the store-room but brooms and dustpans, a few old window shades and some rags Miss Kitty used for dusting the desks. There was no outside door. The only door out of the room opened into the main schoolroom right behind the teacher's desk. The other children would go off the platform down the steps that led directly into the audience; but the ones who spoke later—the big girls and boys—would come through this room as an exit. Also most of the scenery used in the pantomime would have to be dragged in here after the next recitation and song.

To leave the stone where he had found it and go out the door and into the audience was unthinkable. Bickie pushed the thunder-egg back into the corner as far as possible and stood squarely in front of it while the big boys dragged in the boxes and cardboard props from the platform and set them against the back wall. Whenever

To leave the stone where he had found it and go out into
the audience was unthinkable.

anyone spoke to him or looked at him, he fooled with the lantern, turning the flame up or down.

Finally Miss Kitty found him there. "What are you doing in here?" she asked him. "You did very well, Bicknall. We are all proud of you. You needn't be embarrassed. Come on out."

"It's not that." Bickie looked down at his feet. "Howhow did this stone get here?"

"Oh, that?" Miss Kittie laughed. "Mr. Collins brought that one along, with the other stones from his place; but it didn't look like a real stone to me, looked more like a big egg. I didn't think it looked very good with the 'Plymouth Rock' so I pushed it in here. Heavy, isn't it?"

"I think I'll stay in here a while," Bickie told her. He sat down on one of the wooden boxes that had formed the 'Rock.' "My stomach feels funny."

"Too much excitement! " the teacher said. "I'll get you a drink."

But the drink didn't help and of course Miss Kitty had to go on with the program. Bickie knew that within the next hour he was going to face Hake Collins and demand the right to keep his thunder-egg. He knew that he would certainly do it and the feelings in his stomach surprised and frightened him.

"Program too much for you?" Nels Whitney asked as he came through after his song.

Bickie didn't answer.

"Bick's got the stomach-ache," some of the girls giggled.

In spite of his dread and his sick feeling the time hurried by and Bickie, from his corner in the closet, heard the final number of the program—a Goodnight song. Now it was almost time. Hake would come in here for the stones. The boys had brought all the ones on the platform in here. Hake would come to gather them up—yes—yes. He would come any minute now.

It was not Hake but Rudolph, the soldier, and Red-Hog Smith who came looking for Bickie.

"You look kind of peeked, Bick, what's wrong?" Red Hog took him by the shoulder. "Your mother was called out right after your piece and she told me to bring you boys home."

"I suppose someone is sick and they've called her to nurse," Bickie said.

"Why are you hiding here?" Rudolph smiled down at him. "You did fine. Why don't you go out there and let people shake your hand?"

"The thunder-egg! " Bickie spoke in a low voice. "The thunder-egg! "

"What do you mean?" Rudolph looked puzzled.

He pointed to the corner under the lantern where the eggshaped stone sat.

"It's the stone we dug out of our cellar. Don't you remember—the one Uncle Dirk told you about."

The soldier exclaimed in surprise as his eyes darted toward the stone.

"Ain't that the stone I saw at your place?" Red-Hog Smith picked the thunder-egg up in his big hands. He turned it over and over. "A fine stone, I'd say. How come it's here?"

"Hake Collins took it away from us..."

The door opened and Miss Kitty came in. Hake Collins followed her.

"We do appreciate you're going to all that trouble, Mr. Collins," she was saying. "I think the stones looked very nice and we really needed them, don't you think so?"

"Glad to help ye, Ma'am," Hake said with his cackling laugh. "I allus like to be good to folks..."

Then his eye fell on Bickie. He had taken the thunder-egg from Red-Hog and was hugging it tight in his arms.

"Well now, Bick, that there stone is too heavy for a little feller like you." He reached for it.

Bickie backed away. "Don't touch this stone, Hake Collins!" he said. Bickie could hardly believe it was really his own voice. It sounded like John talking. "Don't take my stone again!" Bickie stood between Red-Hog Smith and Hake.

"Well, do tell!" Hake grinned and his mouth lost for a moment its peculiar sucking shape. "This here stone is mine, ain't it, Miss Kitty? I give it to ye for the program, didn't I?" He stood waiting for her to answer.

Miss Kitty looked from Bickie to Hake and then at Red-Hog and the strange soldier in the blue coat. "Yes, Mr. Collins," she said gasping a little. "Yes, it came from your place, I know it did. Why do you claim it, Bicknall?"

"He took it!" Bickie raised his voice, He stole it! Tommie and I...!"

"Look here," Red-Hog glowered at Hake. "This stone belongs to Bick and Tom. I saw it at their place last summer. They dug it up right there in their cellar. How come you think it's yours?"

Hake opened his mouth to answer but Rudolph spoke first. "Is the stone of some value?" he asked.

"Maybe—maybe not." Hake turned his sharp blue eyes on the soldier. "It's none of your put-in. A man has rights. I gotta perteck my property." He tried to twist the stone from Bickie's hands.

The boy resisted and the stone, being rather smooth and rounded was hard to hold. It fell between them and Hake screamed with rage and pain. Oaths and curses filled the air and the angry farmer sat down on one of the boxes to nurse his hurt foot.

"I'll have ye sent to the reform school, ye little wildcat!" he yelled at Bickie.

"Take your shoe off," Rudolph spoke kindly. "Let's see how badly your foot is hurt. That stone is rather heavy."

He unlaced Hake's heavy shoe and gently pulled it off. Hake eased the dirty sock off and then they saw that the stone had fallen on his big toe and given it a bad bruise.

"You'll probably lose your toenail," Rudolph said. "Too bad."

Hake shook his finger at Bickie, "I'll teach you how to behave, you impudent youngun!"

"Now, wait a minute." Rudolph laid his hand on Hake's shoulder, "Just how did you come by this stone?"

"None of your business!" Hake glared at Rudolph. "How about you gettin out of here and lettin me handle this myself. We don't like strangers meddlin!"

Then Red-Hog Smith picked up the stone from the floor where it had fallen. He held it in his hands, "I'll just keep this stone until you prove that it belongs to you, Hake," he said. "So far as I know this belongs to Bick. He says you took it away from him. I'm inclined to believe him."

"That stone came from Californy! I know stones!" Hake's face was purple with anger. "That there's a thunder-egg. When it's cut and polished it might be worth ten dollars and they owe it to me! " His sharp voice had risen to a scream.

Bickie looked from one to another of the faces. His heart beat with wild excitement. Miss Kitty stepped out of the room and closed the door so quietly that the men didn't hear her. Bickie knew they couldn't hear anything the way they were shouting.

"This is the best way, Mr. Collins," Rudolph spoke again. "Let Mr. Smith keep the stone. You wouldn't want to do injustice to an orphan boy I'm sure." He patted the old farmer's slumped shoulder. "I suggest that we take the stone into Marshalltown and have it cut and find out how much it's worth," he looked at Red Hog. "What do you say, Mr. Smith? We can take out the cost of the cutting and whatever the value is...."

"Fine idea," Red-Hog interrupted him. "Whatever the stone is worth you'll get, Hake Collins, but these boys are going to have their stone. Their Uncle fetched it clear from California and he's dead." Red-Hog still held the stone in his hands. His blue eyes flashed in the lantern light, and his big face was very red. "Come on, Bick, we're going home."

"Mr. Collins," Rudolph called back to him, "If you want to be in Marshalltown at eleven o'clock tomorrow morning you will be able to see this stone cut and you will get what we promised you. Otherwise you will never see it again."

The crowd still stood about the door of Ferguson schoolhouse talking and laughing and making such a racket that Bickie was sure none of them had overheard the loud voices in the back storeroom. He looked for Tommie and found him with Pete and Nels. They all followed Red-Hog to the bobsled. He laid the thunderegg on the straw. Then Tommie saw the stone.

"Bickie, Bickie! " he cried out in delight, "It's come back—the thunder-egg! "

The boys snuggled under the buffalo robe and held the stone between them.

Rudolph got in beside them. "That man has done wrong," the soldier told Bickie. "He is fighting a bad conscience. I don't think he will make us any more trouble."

At home the boys got out. They hesitated a minute. Bickie wanted more than anything to take the thunderegg out and carry it into the house, but Red-Hog spoke up.

"I'll just take your stone on home with me," he told them. "I'll have it there in Marshalltown tomorrow and if you boys want to go with me, I'll take you." Then he added in a voice full of unexpected kindness, "I know you fellers would like to have the stone, but I don't trust that Hake. I wouldn't put anything past that sniffling rabbit! "

"Mr. Smith is right," Rudolph assured them, and the two men drove away into the night.

Mother was not home, but John had just come in. He had taken her to spend the night with a sick woman, a couple of miles away.

"John, John!" Bickie called out in a burst of great joy. "Oh, John, the thunder-egg is back!"

"Back?" he looked from one to the other. "Where is it?"

"Red-Hog has it. We are going into Marshalltown tomorrow to have it cut."

"Wait a minute," John sat down by the fire and Bickie told the story of his plan and how it had succeeded.

The boys sat around the kitchen stove until very late. Then John ordered them to bed. "We ought to be all fresh and ready for Marshalltown tomorrow," he said. "I wouldn't miss that for anything."

Bickie slept well that night, so very well that when he saw a figure groping about the floor in the faint moonlight, he knew it was a dream.

"If this Bick hadn't kept his eyes open we never should have discovered it," Rudolph said as he turned the bag upside down.

Chapter 13

The Thunder-Egg Is Cut

SINCE THANKSGIVING vacation had already begun, the boys were free to go along to Marshalltown. Even Mother decided to go. When Red-Hog Smith came by to pick them up in his bobsled they were all ready.

At eleven o'clock the whole Ross family stood talking with Red-Hog Smith and Rudolph, the soldier in the stone-cutter's shop. The man, who owned the little shop, had a fine collection of polished stones. Now he stood behind his wooden counter and studied the thunder-egg before him.

"It's unusually heavy," he said, looking it over and lifting it. "Must have a core of solid agate."

"Have you seen others as heavy as this one?" John asked.

"Oh, yes, if the agate core comes out close to the outer shell of a thunder-egg it will be quite heavy." John and Rudolph looked at each other. Bickie stood hardly breathing. Mother's lips were pressed tight together and there was a bright look in her eyes. Tommie looked from one face to another as though he was afraid he might miss a look or a word.

Red-Hog stood looking at the thunder-egg. He turned to Mother, "I swa'an, if I didn't think Hake might try to break into your place last night to look for this stone. He was that mad…"

"The lock on our kitchen door was pulled loose this morning," John said. "But I think one of the boys did it...."

Then Hake Collins came in. He limped a little from his sore toe, but he greeted them all with a hearty "Good morning!"

"Well, why do we wait?" he looked around at the others. "Let's see this here stone cut. You will pay, of course?" He looked at Rudolph.

"Yes, Mr. Collins,, I will pay for having the stone sawed in two. That will be a dollar and a half." Rudolph motioned toward the stonecutter, "When this gentleman cuts the stone and tells us its value, we will settle up right here."

The owner of the shop placed the stone in cutting position and the saw began to make a groove in it. There was a lot of noise with the grinding of the teeth as they bit into the thunder-egg and nobody talked. Everyone was intent on the stone.

"It's taking longer than usual," the man said, pouring a little more water on the cutting edge of the saw. It is even harder than I thought. Then he went back to his saw again. It was hard work.

When the two severed halves fell apart, a sigh went up from all who watched. Where was the gold? the money? Bickie wasn't sure that he had really expected some fabulous wealth to be hidden inside the stone. It looked very ordinary, now, laid with its two halves side by side on the wooden counter.

Rudolph looked at John and John looked at Mother. Tommie opened his mouth, but Bickie clapped his hand over Tommie's mouth. He was afraid Tommie might blurt out what they had talked about the thunder-egg and Hake Collins would hear.

"It is an unusually fine specimen," the man told them. "It should Polish beautifully, but of course that will take several days." He wiped the sweat from his face with his jacket sleeve.

"What value do you set on the stone as it sets right now?" Rudolph asked.

"Oh, I should say each half is worth at least four dollars and a half." The man picked up one of the cut pieces and examined it carefully. "One couldn't say for certain until they are polished, but I think that's a fair estimate."

Rudolph pulled out his wallet. He counted out a dollar and a half and paid for the cutting of the stone. Then he counted out seven dollars and fifty cents and handed it to Hake.

"I'd like a receipt for that, Mr. Collins," he said. "And I want the receipt to say that this amount is deducted from what Mrs. Ross owes you."

Hake took a scrap of wrapping paper from his pocket and wrote out the receipt in a cramped, tight hand.

When Hake was gone they stepped outside the shop. Bickie held one-half of the thunder-egg and Tommie held the other. Rudolph looked down at Bickie, "I think you have something pretty nice there. Later when you can afford to get them polished you will get lots of pleasure out of looking at them. You will remember Uncle Dirk." He buttoned up his blue coat. "You may pay me back the nine dollars when you are able."

Red-Hog Smith left them and walked off in the direction of Forepaugh's General Store.

"Well," John said with a deep sigh, "This puts us right back where we started doesn't it?" Rudolph stood scratching his head. "I'm sure I'm not mistaken in what Dirk Himes told me. He said, 'Find the stone.'"

"Surely he wouldn't have worried about the value of this thunderegg and made it the subject of his last wish," Mother said.

"I don't think so either, Mrs. Ross." Rudolph looked troubled. "There must be some other stone. We will have to look some more. We will have to dig all over that cellar floor. Perhaps there is another stone there."

"Come out tomorrow, then," John said as they parted in front of the stonecutter's shop in Marshalltown.

They all followed Red-Hog down to Forepaugh's store and spent an hour or more enjoying the delectable smells and wonderful sights. Mother even bought a wooden pail of jelly and some candy for the boys. It was altogether a glorious day.

The snow lay two and a half feet on the level and more fell that night, but the following morning dawned bright and sunny. Bickie and Tommie dressed in their warmest things. It was the day before Thanksgiving. They hurried out to help John clear away the snow from the cellar floor. Bickie even brought Mother's kitchen broom and swept it clean. By the time Rudolph came they were ready to start digging.

Mother heated water in the big wash boiler and filled the top of the stove with kettles full of water. She filled the reservoir on the side of the stove.

"This hot water may help to thaw out that frozen ground," she told the boys.

The soil under the cellar floor was not frozen so deep as that on the surface of the ground. They poured boiling water along one side and were soon able to get through the three or four inches of frozen dirt. After that it went rather well. They could get their shovels down under the frozen crust. It was muddy, dirty work. Bickie and Tommie sat on the sandstone wall and watched.

The men threw one spadeful after another against the wall behind them. The area was not more than twenty feet square and the two men digging steadily soon got to the middle. There were no stones at all. There was nothing!

The men stopped to rest, "It's no use," John said. "There's nothing here, I'm sure."

"Well, we've started. Let's finish. It won't take long." Rudolph threw a spadeful of muddy earth back toward the wall. Bickie saw a black thing drop against the red sandstone. It looked like the limp body of a rat or mole or some other small animal. He climbed down and went to look at it.

He picked it up. It was a small leather bag, blackened by the mud and water, wet and soggy. It was tied with a thong of dirty black leather. It looked like a leather shoestring. The thing felt heavy in his hand and it was getting his mitten dirty.

"Look!" he held up the leather bag for all of them to see, "What's this?"

John and Rudolph looked up. They stopped digging. They came over to where Bickie stood. Tommie climbed down from the wall. Rudolph took the small wet pouch in his hand. He got out his pocket knife and slit the leather string that tied it shut. The boys stood watching him in almost unbearable suspense.

Then Rudolph put the knife back in his pocket. "I think before we see what's in this bag, we should take it in the house and let your mother have a look at it. I feel pretty sure this is what we are looking for and it belongs to her."

Solemnly and with a wildly beating heart, Bickie followed the others into the house and heard as in a dream while Rudolph explained to Mother what they had done and how Bickie had seen the little black object thrown against the wall.

"If this Bick hadn't kept his eyes open we should never have discovered it," Rudolph said as he turned the bag upside down and spilled the contents on the kitchen table.

No one spoke for a moment. Dozens of small nuggets and some larger ones sprawled across the table top—pure gold! The old Seth Thomas clock looked down and Bickie heard its loud tick pounding through the quietness of the room.

"Mother, Mother!" Tommie spoke first. "What are they? Are they stones?"

"No, Tom," Rudolph laid a hand on his shoulder, "This is gold. This is raw gold from California. It is in nuggets just like the miners found it in the sand and streams there."

"Is this what Uncle Dirk meant" Bickie felt quiet and churchy inside.

"I'm sure it is," Rudolph said.

"It must have been buried right underneath the thunder-egg," John spoke up. "That's why he told you to 'Find the stone.'"

They looked at the gold for quite a while and still Mother had not said a word. Finally she asked in a low voice, "What is its value. Can you estimate?" she looked at Rudolph.

"I should say roughly between fifteen hundred and two thousand dollars," Rudolph told her. "I have had some experience with these things."

"We can build our home again." She drew a deep breath and reached out to draw the two little boys into her arms.

"We can pay off Hake Collins," John added.

"We can buy seed corn for planting, and seed potatoes too." Bickie remembered.

"We can have jelly every day and pumpkin pie and beef stew," Tommie sang out in a joyous voice.

"And what can we do for you, our good friend." Mother held out her hand to Rudolph. "Without you this would never have come to us."

"Let me come to visit you when the new house is built. Let me eat and sleep there for a day or two and let me see the two halves of the thunder-egg all polished and setting in the boys' room."

He laughed and slapped John on the back.

When the nuggets were weighed and sold, their value was a little more than Rudolph figured. John secured the mortgage money and put it in Hake Collins' hand, not forgetting to ask for a proper receipt.

There came a day when the boys brought home the polished halves of the thunder-egg. A beautiful design appeared in the glassy surface of the agate.

"It looks like white wings over green water," Tommie said.

"It looks like lots and lots of angels," Bickie told Mother.

"Yes, it does." She looked long at the lovely stones. "We will keep these where we can always see them. They will remind us of God's wings of mercy that were over us in all our troubles."

Neighbors came to help build a new house on the old red sandstone foundation. It looked a great deal like the home that burned. Two little green windows looked out from under the gable and when springtime came again, a yellow rose vine climbed over a new porch.

Sharna of Rocky Bay

Alice Mertie Underhill tells the story of a young girl who spent her childhood amidst the cold, rocky coves of Rocky Bay.

The Adventures of Kado

Alice Underhill's true-to-life story of a native boy and how he grows from a regular savage's child, to an influential Christian.

Other Titles from TEACH Services, Inc.

Treasure From the Haunted Pagoda

Eric B. Hare tells the way in which God prepared the 'special place' where a little boy grew to manhood among the superstitious tales of devil-worshipers.

Choma—A Boy of Central Africa

Ella Robinson's character-building story of a young African boy living in a large village. When missionaries visit the village he learns about God, the Bible.

The Queen's Gold

Norma R. Youngberg's
exciting story of a young
man shipwrecked and raised
by the natives until…
the pirates come!

The Tiger of Bitter Valley

A boy comes of age in this
gripping tale of good vs. evil
by Norma R. Youngberg.

Other Titles from TEACH Services, Inc.

Miracle in Borneo

Norma R. Youngberg tells a
story that emphasizes the
importance of native evange-
lists in overseas missions.

Miracle of the Song

Damin encounters danger
and discovers that a deep
faith is more powerful than
any great warrior in this
timeless classic by author
Norma R. Youngberg.

We invite you to view the complete
selection of titles we publish at:

www.TEACHServices.com

or write or email us your praises,
reactions, or thoughts about this
or any other book we publish at:

TEACH Services, Inc.
P U B L I S H I N G
www.TEACHServices.com
P.O. Box 954
Ringgold, GA 30736

info@TEACHServices.com

TEACH Services, Inc. titles may be purchased in bulk for
educational, business, fund-raising, or sales promotional use. For
information, please e-mail

BulkSales@TEACHServices.com.

Finally, if you are interested in seeing
your own book in print, please contact us at

publishing@teachservices.com.

We would be happy to review your manuscript for free.